With thirty seconds to go, all that remained of the wedding dress's skirt were ragged scraps of silk that fell to midthigh on the most fabulous pair of golden legs Marcelo had ever seen.

His hands fisted on the material as the compulsion surged through him to grip her curvy hips and press his face into the cleavage peeking up from where the silk and lace of the dress dipped like a heart.

Never in his wildest dreams had he imagined his damsel in distress would be so damn sexy.

"Eyes to face, Berruti," she scolded, holding her middle and index fingers like claws to her eyes.

He gazed up at the beautiful face. "You know who I am?"

She rolled her eyes. "I wouldn't let just any old riffraff rescue me, you know."

Dio, he wanted to kiss that smart, perfectly plump mouth, but with time pressing, he resisted, instead jumping to his feet and taking hold of her hand.

Scandalous Royal Weddings

Marriages to make front-page news!

Raised on the Mediterranean island kingdom of Ceres, Princes Amadeo and Marcelo and Princess Alessia want for nothing. But with their life of luxury comes an impeccable reputation to uphold. Any hint of a scandal could turn the eyes of the world on them...and force them down the royal aisle! Their lives may be lived in the spotlight, but only one person will have the power to truly see them...

When Prince Marcelo rescues Clara from a forced wedding, he simultaneously risks a diplomatic crisis and his heart.

Read on in
Crowning His Kidnapped Princess
Available now!

Billionaire Gabriel may fix scandals for a living, but his night with Princess Alessia creates a scandal of their own when she discovers she's pregnant!

And Prince Amadeo must face a stranger at the altar, when convenient royal wedding bells chime.

Both coming soon!

Don't miss this scandalous trilogy by
Michelle Smart!

Michelle Smart

CROWNING HIS KIDNAPPED PRINCESS

HARLEQUIN

PRESENTS

HARLEQUIN®
PRESENTS™

ISBN-13: 978-1-335-58366-6

Crowning His Kidnapped Princess

Copyright © 2022 by Michelle Smart

Harlequin Enterprises ULC
22 Adelaide St. West, 41st Floor
Toronto, Ontario M5H 4E3, Canada
www.Harlequin.com

Printed in U.S.A.

Michelle Smart's love affair with books started when she was a baby and would cuddle them in her cot. A voracious reader of all genres, she found her love of romance established when she stumbled across her first Harlequin book at the age of twelve. She's been reading them—and writing them—ever since. Michelle lives in Northamptonshire, England, with her husband and two young Smarties.

Books by Michelle Smart

Harlequin Presents

Stranded with Her Greek Husband
Claiming His Baby at the Altar

Billion-Dollar Mediterranean Brides

The Forbidden Innocent's Bodyguard
The Secret Behind the Greek's Return

The Delgado Inheritance

The Billionaire's Cinderella Contract
The Cost of Claiming His Heir

Christmas with a Billionaire

Unwrapped by Her Italian Boss

Visit the Author Profile page
at Harlequin.com for more titles.

CHAPTER ONE

CLARA SINCLAIR PACED her prison cell. If she was feeling charitable she'd admit her cell, which easily measured thirty by thirty feet and came with its own four-poster bed, an adjoining private bathroom and had three high bay windows with views straight onto the palace's private harbour, was the kind of prison cell most incarcerated criminals would kill for. In some cases, again. Her current prison outfit was rather flashier than what an inmate would expect to wear too, being made of white silk with an overlay of white lace. If she hadn't been forcibly straitjacketed into it, she might think it beautiful.

She almost wished her female guards were still in the cell with her. Then she could have the satisfaction of calling them every nasty name she could dredge up and watch their faces turn puce. But no, they'd all gone off to get themselves dolled up for the Monte Cleure event of the decade—Clara's marriage to King Dominic of the House of Fernandez. Her other prison guards, two beefy men, were stationed on the other side of the door as they'd been since the first time she'd tried to escape. Still, she hadn't shouted at them in at least twenty minutes, so she hammered on the door, and yelled, 'May your bedsheets be cursed with ginormous blood-sucking bedbugs, you *pigs*!'

As with every other insult and curse she'd aimed at them these past two weeks, she was rewarded with silence.

The clock on her wall chimed the quarter hour. Goody. Only fifteen minutes to go before she was married off to the biggest pig of them all, the King himself. And she couldn't even make a scene in the royal chapel, not with the threat to Bob's life. Dominic would do it too. And probably take great pleasure from it.

What kind of evil bastard gave a woman a puppy and then used it as a weapon to threaten her with? The man she was marrying in fifteen minutes, that's who. For now, Bob was safe and fast asleep in his basket. He would remain safe only if she said, 'I do,' without punching the groom. Or the priest. Or any of the guests.

Until she'd arrived in Monte Cleure and found herself held against her will, Clara had never hit anyone in her life, nor felt the urge to, not even her half-brother, who'd treated her like doggy-do since their father died and who was equally responsible for her predicament as the King himself.

What kind of evil bastard sold his own sister? Her brother, the Honourable Andrew Sinclair, that's who.

She banged her fist on the door again. 'You're going to burn in hell for this, do you know that?' she shouted before dramatically flinging herself onto the floor.

Bob woke up and padded over to curl onto her lap.

Stroking his soft head, she felt no compulsion to cry. She was too angry for tears and, in any case, tears solved nothing. Clara had learned that as a small child when her tears had failed to bring her mother back to life. She'd also learned that moaning and bewailing your bad fortune solved nothing either.

If she was going to escape, she needed to get a move on.

What had she missed? She had ten minutes left before they dragged her to the chapel.

Think!

The fireplace had been bricked up within minutes of them finding her wriggling up it. The air vent covers had been superglued in place as a precaution. Opening a window and screaming for help had resulted in Bob being dangled out of the window with the threat to drop him in the private harbour forty feet below.

She would make Dominic's life a living hell. She would be the wife from Hades. If he thought he could bully her into compliance then he had another…

A tapping sound jolted her out of her furious musings and she raised her head sharply. There was a face at the window.

Certain she was imagining it, she blinked then blinked again. The face was still there.

It was a handsome face, the mouth curved into a wide grin, the tilting head indicating for her to hurry and open the window.

Scrambling to her feet, Clara almost tripped over the train of her wedding dress in her haste to reach the handsome stranger.

As she tugged at the sash window, she thought vaguely that there was something familiar about the handsome stranger but the joy of imminent rescue overrode it, as did the difficulty she was experiencing in opening the ruddy thing.

Dominic hadn't had it glued stuck, had he? She couldn't think when, not when she'd been confined to the room for two whole weeks, half of which had been spent with her head stuck out of this very window wondering if it was possible to make herself a rope out of her bedsheets and escape that way. She would have done it too if her female guards, or 'companions,' as Dominic called them, had left her for longer than twenty minutes at a time.

Just as she was thinking she'd have to smash the glass, there was some give. A bit more muscle and up the window rose.

Yes!

'Hello,' she said, grinning broadly, placing where she knew the handsome face from. 'Are you the cavalry?'

Ice-blue eyes sparkled. Straight white teeth flashed. '*Ciao, bella.* Would you like a ride in my helicopter?'

Marcelo Berruti swung himself into the room and took stock of the beautiful young woman smiling at him like he was Father Christmas. Adrenaline pumped hard through him, an excitement he hadn't experienced since his military days. As a child he'd often scaled the walls of the castle he called home imagining himself a knight in shining armour rescuing a damsel in distress. Who'd have known he'd reach the age of thirty and do it for real?

This particular damsel didn't look in the least distressed. If anything, she looked like she was about to burst out laughing and he instinctively placed a finger to her lips.

'Shh,' he whispered, and pointed at the door.

Large dark brown eyes brimming with glee widened like a naughty schoolgirl caught smoking by an indulgent teacher, and he remembered how Alessia had admiringly described Clara

Sinclair as the naughty girl of their exclusive boarding school. Alessia had failed to mention Clara's beauty, and he allowed himself a moment to sweep his eyes over the heart-shaped face with the high cheekbones, the soft plump lips his finger was currently pressed against and the perfectly straight nose, and down to the curvy body with the full breasts wrapped in a wedding dress. The picture-perfect sight was finished with her dark blond hair swept up in an elegant knot.

Slender fingers suddenly grabbed his hand and moved his finger from her mouth.

'Are you here to ogle me or rescue me?' she asked in an exaggerated whisper.

'Can't a man do both?'

'Not when I'm about to be dragged out of this room and frogmarched down the aisle in five minutes.'

'That is a very good point.' Stepping away from her, Marcelo carried the chair from her dressing table to the door and quietly but securely placed it under the handle before looking at his watch and turning back to her. 'We have two minutes. Do you have anything you can change into?'

'In two minutes?'

'One minute and fifty seconds.'

She held her palms out and shrugged. 'It

took an hour for them to pin me into this stupid thing.'

'Scissors?'

'Not allowed them in case I stab someone,' she explained cheerfully.

He dropped to his knees in front of her and took hold of the lace at the hem of the dress. 'Stay still.'

'What are you doing?'

'This…' Looking up at her beautiful face, he tore the lace.

She pulled a mock shocked face. 'But, sir, we've only just met.'

He grinned, put a hand to her hip and spun her around to help the lace rip until it was removed all the way to her hips.

In the distance came the telltale sound of his helicopter nearing them. Now for the silk of the dress. This proved harder to tear into than the lace.

'Use your teeth?' she suggested.

He pulled his own mock shocked face. 'But, madam, we've only just met.' And then he proceeded to do exactly as she'd suggested.

With thirty seconds to go, all that remained of the skirt of the wedding dress was ragged scraps of silk falling to mid-thigh on the most fabulous pair of golden legs Marcelo had ever seen. His hands fisted on the material he still had hold of as the compulsion to grip the curvy hips and press his face into the cleavage on display where the silk and lace of the dress dipped like a heart surged through him.

Never in his wildest dreams had he imagined his damsel in distress would be so damn sexy.

'Eyes to face, Berruti,' she scolded, holding her fore and index fingers like claws to her eyes.

He gazed up at the beautiful face. 'You know who I am?'

She rolled her eyes. 'I don't let any old riffraff rescue me, you know.'

Dio, he wanted to kiss that smart, perfectly plump mouth but, with time pressing, he resisted, instead jumping to his feet and taking hold of her hand.

'How are you with heights?' he asked. The helicopter now hovered over them, its rotors so loud whispering was no longer an option.

'I guess we're about to find out?'

A rope appeared in front of the window at the same moment the handle of the door rattled.

'Time's up,' he said. 'Let's go.'

'Hold on a sec.' She yanked her hand from his and knelt down to scoop up a small chocolate-brown furry thing Marcelo hadn't noticed before.

'You can't take that,' he said as loud shouting and hammering penetrated through the door.

'I can't leave him. Dominic will kill him.'

Marcelo pointed at the dangling rope. 'We can't escape on that with a dog.'

Utterly unperturbed, Clara looked down at her cleavage. 'Rip this. Quickly.'

'What?'

There was a loud crash against the door.

'Quickly,' she said with the first hint of impatience. 'Rip it. Just a few inches.'

Realising what she intended, Marcelo put his hand on the top of the dress and tore it apart so it opened to reveal ample breasts hidden behind an ugly plain white bra.

Seeing he'd noticed, Clara smiled wickedly. 'You should see my knickers.' Then she carefully put the puppy down her dress in the space he'd just made.

'Lucky puppy,' he drawled. 'Can we go now?'

'Go on then.'

There was yet another loud smash against the door as he jumped onto the windowsill. Marcelo grabbed the rope. Clara seemed not to need instruction, nimbly climbing up beside him and wrapping her arms around his neck.

'Pleased to meet you,' she said, gazing up at his face with a grin.

He couldn't help grinning back as he wound the rope securely around them. 'Hold tight.'

'No, *you* hold tight.'

Laughing, he hooked an arm around her

waist, stuck a thumb up at the helicopter, then held her tightly as they were lifted into the air.

Clara's stomach dipped and then she was weightless, flying, warm air rushing through and around her. She kept her fear locked tightly away, as tightly as she held to her old school friend's macho brother, and kept her stare firmly fixed on his face, feeding off the supreme confidence written on it that said they would be lifted to safety. She would not allow herself to think that, should his knot-making skills be subpar, they were both liable to plummet to certain death… Oh, dear. She'd just thought it.

Think of poor Bob nestled between her breasts, she told herself. Judging by the way his sharp little claws were digging into her skin, the poor mite was terrified.

A jolt on the rope made her stomach dip again, and she squeezed her eyes shut and leaned her forehead into Marcelo's hard chest and prayed their pressed bodies was barrier enough to stop Bob scrambling out and, conversely, not too smothering that they suffocated him.

Before guilt that she'd done the wrong thing in bringing the puppy with them could set too deeply, hands grabbed hold of her and she was being roughly manhandled onto the helicopter.

Relief surged through her like a frothing tsunami, and she would have rolled onto her back from the sheer force of it if she wasn't bound to the hunk who'd taken it on himself to rescue her.

They'd made it! She was free.

The noise of the rotors wasn't loud enough to drown the thrash of her heartbeats ringing in her ears. She tried to catch a breath before opening her eyes. She had to blink a number of times before her vision cleared and she could attempt to get her bearings. The helicopter itself was huge and looked more military than civilian. Two men dressed in military fatigues were knelt beside them working to untie the knots binding her to Marcelo.

It came to Clara in a rush that she was trussed up on the floor of a helicopter with the Prince of Ceres and with a puppy scrambling frantically for release from the confines of her cleavage. The relief and absurdity of it all became too much and, unable to control it, Clara burst into peals of laughter. She was still laughing when the rope slackened, still laughing when she managed to sit up, still laughing as she carefully pulled Bob out of her cleavage. But then Bob licked her cheek and her laughter merged into tears that she couldn't control either. Through the sobbing laughter was an awareness that three macho men were warily studying her, no doubt alarmed at this display of female hysteria, a notion that only made her laugh and cry harder.

Her eighteen days on Monte Cleure, sixteen

spent as a captive, had put her through the emotional wringer but she'd refused to succumb to distress, focusing everything on the anger she'd need as fuel to escape even when escape had seemed hopeless, and she sobbed and laughed until everything she'd suppressed was purged.

It took so long for her to regain control of herself that they'd probably left Monte Cleure airspace before she'd wiped the last tear away. Needing a tissue, she looked at the ragged remnants of her wedding dress and ripped off another piece of silk to blow her nose.

Then she looked at Marcelo. He was sat on the cold metal helicopter floor beside her, an air of amusement mingling with the concern on his face. During her bout of hysteria, Bob had plonked himself onto his lap, and a hand that was practically the same size as the puppy gently stroked his head.

Scrunching the makeshift hankie into a ball, Clara stuffed it into her bra. 'That has to be the world's most expensive handkerchief,' she said.

Thick black eyebrows drew in together.

'This dress cost Dominic a hundred thousand euros,' she explained before another short burst of laughter flew from her lips. Her purge of emotions had been cathartic. Now she felt as emotionally high as she was physically in this military grade helicopter. 'I might send it to him as a keepsake of our time together.'

Marcelo had seen feminine tears many times in his life. His sister, Alessia, could turn them on like taps. Most girlfriends had proven themselves excellent at summoning tears to get their own way—one lover, Gianna, had thrown herself at his feet weeping and wailing when he'd ended their relationship, something he always reflected on with bemusement considering they were only together a couple of months. Bemusement was his default emotion with female tears along with a certain amount of bracing himself for the sad eyes and woebegone expression that always followed. There was none of that with Clara Sinclair.

Her tears had been spectacular. The chokes of laughter the sobs had been interspersed with had only added to the spectacle. And then it was done, and now she was sat cross-legged on the helicopter floor, dark brown eyes puffy, her face streaked with mascara but with the expression of someone who'd already put the tears behind her. The adventure from the palace into the helicopter had made her hair come loose, windswept long dark blond hair splayed all around her.

'Better?' he asked, already knowing what the answer would be.

'Much, thank you. And thank you for rescuing me.' She blew a strand of hair off her mouth and grinned. 'I owe you one.'

'It was my pleasure.' And the knowledge of

this incredibly sexy creature being in his debt only heightened the pleasure. She was fascinating.

She stretched her glorious legs out and hooked her ankles together. She had pretty feet, he noted. The puppy jumped off his lap and onto hers.

She fussed over the puppy then turned her attention sharply back to him. 'I've only just noticed—you're wearing a tuxedo.'

'I am,' he agreed.

Her plump lips puckered and wriggled. 'I thought superheroes were supposed to wear spandex or something? And their pants over their tights?'

Laughing at the imagery, he shook his head. 'I'm wearing a tuxedo because I dressed for a wedding.'

Her eyes widened and she gave a bark of laughter. 'You were a guest?'

'I accepted as a representative of the Berruti royal family.'

'Amazing. And so sneaky!'

He shrugged as if the effort of rescuing her was nothing at all. 'The invitation came three days after my sister showed me your message.' The message had been as forthright as the woman who'd written it:

The King of Monte Cleure has imprisoned me and is forcing me to marry him. SEND HELP!!!

Marcelo had assumed it was a joke. Even Alessia had been unconvinced of its truthfulness—it was well known publicly that Dominic was searching for a royal bride, and Clara Sinclair's reputation preceded her—but when Alessia's reply went unanswered, doubt had set in and his sister had proceeded to give him earache about rescuing her old wayward friend. And then the wedding invitation had arrived by courier and Marcelo suddenly found a way to get one up on a man he loathed and who treated women like dirt and who gave royal families a bad name, *and* appease his sister all in one shot. Also, he'd been bored. An injection of excitement in a life that had been mind-numbingly predictable since his military career had come to a premature end had proved irresistible.

The initial plan for his old army friends to undertake the rescue mission while he sat in the royal chapel with his credentials as a bona-fide guest his alibi, a last-minute vision of himself sweeping in like a heroic knight in shining armour and the surge of adrenaline the thought had sent through him had also proved irresistible.

Marcelo hadn't had a rush like that in three

years. He could still feel the after-effects buzzing in his veins.

'I wasn't sure if the message went out,' Clara said, thrilled that this one action had been successful. All her other efforts to escape King Pig had been abject failures. 'Dominic caught me writing it and stole my phone while I was pressing send.'

'Who did you send it to?'

'Everyone in my contacts.' All ten of them. Alessia, her only friend from her school days, had been her biggest hope. The other contacts had been her aunt in Australia, who no doubt would have called Andrew and been fobbed off by him, some work colleagues and an old lady who'd adopted one of the dogs from the animal shelter Clara worked at and who would call if her arthritis got too bad and she needed Clara to walk Buster for her.

'Clever.'

'Was there an international outcry?' she asked, more in hope than expectation.

'I'm afraid not.'

Her face scrunched in disappointment, making Marcelo laugh again. 'Going to tell me how you got yourself into this predicament?'

Her expression changed to indignant. 'Got *myself* into it? Nice bit of victim blaming there.'

'Clumsy wording,' he said by way of an apology. 'Go on, tell me. I'm curious.'

'Hmm…' Her lips puckered and wriggled again and then she sat up straighter and inched herself back so her back rested against the hard bench running along the helicopter's far side. 'Well, my brother asked me to go to Monte Cleure on his behalf to sell the amazing properties of the sparkling English wine he's producing on the family estate to the King of Monte Cleure. With me so far?'

'Indeed.'

'Great.' She flashed a smile. 'So I agreed to his request and off I popped to Monte Cleure and I was welcomed like a princess. *Amazing* hospitality. Honestly. Amazing. I was put up in the palace and dined on the *best* food, I had access to the spa and swimming pools, everything. Still with me?'

'Yes,' he agreed drily, although it was rather difficult concentrating on the words she was saying when the lips forming the words were so succulent.

'Good. Because this is where it gets interesting. On my second night, the king proposed to me.'

He arched a brow.

She nodded sagely in response. 'That was my reaction too. I only just stopped myself from laughing in his face, but I told him the truth, that I don't want to get married. I was quite pleased with myself for not insulting him with my refusal.'

'You weren't tempted?'

'Have you seen him? The man's a pig.'

'He's also a king,' he pointed out.

She gave a short rise of her shoulders. 'So what? Doesn't stop him being a pig. He even eats like a pig. It's disgusting.'

Having suffered a number of functions where Dominic had been in attendance, Marcelo could only agree with this assessment of the man's eating habits. 'What was his reaction to your refusal?'

'He was very understanding. All piggy sweetness and light.' Her face darkened. 'The next morning, he joined me for breakfast and referred to me as his fiancée. I told him again that I didn't want to get married and he just laughed. When I went to collect my stuff to leave, my suitcase had been ransacked and my passport and purse stolen, and then King Pig came to my room and told me I was going to marry him whether I liked it or not and that I'd better get used to the idea or there would be consequences. The next day he brought Bob to my room and told me he was the first of many gifts I would receive if I was a *good girl*.' Distaste dripped in every syllable.

'Bob?'

She nodded at the puppy curled on her lap.

'He knew how much I love animals and thought a dog would make me want to marry him. Seriously, the man's on another planet.'

'Why you? Did he ever say?'

'Oh, yes,' she said matter-of-factly. 'He wants to marry me because I have royal blood in my veins—that it's heavily diluted doesn't matter apparently—and because I'm a virgin.'

CHAPTER TWO

FOR THE FIRST time since he'd appeared at her window, Marcelo looked nonplussed. 'I beg your pardon?' he said. 'You're a virgin?'

'Yep,' she answered cheerfully. Clara was not in the least embarrassed about her virgin state. 'Apparently a virgin is more of a guarantee that any child will be his. Because, obviously, once a woman's experienced sex she turns into a raging nymphomaniac and has to have it with any man within a ten-mile radius and is so overtaken by lust she forgets to use contraception, especially when she's out there having her wicked way with all those men who aren't her husband.'

Marcelo just stared at her. She became aware that the men who'd hauled them onto the helicopter were staring at her from their seats on the bench too. They all appeared dumbfounded.

'What's wrong?' she asked, looking from one to the other. 'You're not married and now worried your wives are out there shacking up with your nearest neighbour, are you? Honestly, that was just Dominic's tiny, paranoid mind coming into play. I mean, I don't know, maybe your wives *are* having affairs but if they are, I assure you, it's not because they're nymphomaniacs but because they're unhappy in your marriage so my advice would be to fix any unhappiness. Women like to feel loved and appreciated. And wanted. Flowers are always appreciated too but I wouldn't recommend using them as a form of apology—if you need to apologise and show how remorseful you are, a grovelling apology on bended knee works a treat.'

'Does it?' Marcelo asked faintly.

Her face scrunched as she shrugged. 'Well, that's what I'd prefer if my husband upset me but I don't suppose I can speak for other women, and it's all a bit moot because I'm never going to get married. I'd quite like a man to get on bended knee and produce a grovelling apology though.'

'For what?'

Clara considered the question. 'My father for not protecting me? My brother for selling me to a pig? Yes. Those things warrant grovelling apologies. But it's not quite the same thing, is it?' She considered it some more. 'No, on second thoughts, grovelling on bended knee to your daughter or sister feels a bit wrong. Those kind of grovels should be left for lovers to do. And my father's dead so I'm going to have to wait until I join him in hell before I get any apology off him, and Andrew wouldn't know an apology if it slapped him in the face.'

The stupid thing was that until she'd received her brother's beautifully written letter—Andrew was a traditionalist—inviting her to dinner, Clara hadn't cared that she was estranged from him…or, more truthfully, that he was estranged from her. Older than her by two decades, Andrew had always treated her with disdain, like she was a nuisance to be tolerated, even when he'd been her legal guardian. He'd resented her as a child for being the catalyst of his parents' divorce, their father leaving his mother for Clara's mother, and as she'd grown older she'd grown into an embarrassment to him. Before that dinner invitation arrived, she hadn't seen him in the four years since he'd turned up at her flat on her eighteenth birthday, not with a present for her but with details of a savings account her mother had set up for her when she'd been born. The last deposit had been made when Clara was four. There was enough in it for her to replace her sagging fourth-hand sofa with a less sagging second-hand one, little enough money for Clara to know her father had kept his second wife's spending tightly controlled.

She hadn't realised until she'd received Andrew's letter and her heart had felt fit to burst that she'd nestled a secret hope her pompous brother could look past the circumstances of her birth and the personality traits he found so insufferable, and want a relationship with her. She guessed that's why it hadn't occurred to her that what she'd taken to be his attempt at a reproachment between them had a malevolent ulterior motive.

Andrew's loathing of her ran deeper than she'd known.

Something flickered in Marcelo's ice-blue eyes. 'You think your brother sold you to Dominic?'

'I don't know in what form he was paid for it—he doesn't need the money as he's loaded, so probably wants the cachet of being brother-in-law to a king—but yes, he sold me to him.' Andrew had tricked her and sold her to a monster. Feeling her belly roil and churn, she squashed the pointless pain down and gave her attention to something much worthier: Marcelo's hair, which he was currently running his fingers through.

It was nice hair, Clara decided. And much nicer to focus on than allowing her brain to think about her brother. It hurt much less too. Almost black in contrast to those ice-blue eyes—mind you, the ring around the iris was as black as the pupils, adding a different dimension to them—Marcelo's hair was long at the front and currently flopping over his forehead thanks to being ravaged by the wind. Marcelo Berruti had the look of someone who took great pride in his personal grooming, the black beard covering the square jaw just the right side of designer stubble. She wondered if it was soft to the touch or bristly and then thought that that was a thought she'd never pondered before. Interesting…

Marcelo Berruti was interesting. Physically. If interesting was a substitute for drop-dead gorgeous. Because that's what he was. Drop-dead gorgeous. Even his mouth was sexy, all full yet firm. And wide. She wondered what those lips would feel like against hers, which was also interesting as Clara had never wondered that about any man before. Now that the shock of being airlifted onto a helicopter had abated, she could admit that it had felt very nice being held against his solid body.

'Have you got a girlfriend?' she asked on impulse.

The kissable lips parted then closed. He blinked then gave a short shake of his head. 'Are you for real?'

'Of course.' She held an arm out to him. 'See? Touch me. I'm as real as you are.'

He looked from her extended arm to her face and gave another short shake of his head. 'Do you have a filter for your mouth?'

'No, but I probably need one. Dominic did threaten to gag me a number of times.'

'What stopped him?'

'He was scared I would bite him.'

If Marcelo shook his head again he would give himself whiplash. This woman though...

He'd known she was a handful. Alessia had told him that much, how the teachers at their strict school had grown so exasperated at having to continually sanction her that Clara had been placed in a bedroom with Alessia in the hope his sister, a year older than her, would be a good influence. That arrangement had lasted until Clara's expulsion. Alessia had confided in him, 'There were so many rumours flying around about the expulsion being to do with a fire alarm going off in an exam but that didn't make sense to me and nothing was confirmed. Whatever it was, she was a complete handful and drove the teachers nuts but, for me, there was something inherently loveable about her that made you want to protect her from herself.'

He didn't think he'd met a woman in less need of protection in his life. She might have the looks of someone who'd just stepped out of a Botticelli painting but that runaway mouth would drive a saint to losing its patience. And he'd only known her an hour!

'He would never have controlled you,' he murmured.

She sighed and rubbed her fingers through Bob's fur. 'He would have used this little one to control me. He really had done his homework

on me, but between you and me…and them…'
She indicated his two paratrooper friends who'd
come along to help and were clearly listening,
agog, to their conversation. 'I think he'd run out
of options. He took the throne a couple of years
ago and needed to start breeding, but every eli-
gible princess or duchess or whatever in Europe
turned him down. I personally think he was a
bit desperate when he decided I was the perfect
woman to be his queen.'

Marcelo's own sister had been one of the el-
igible princesses to turn the King down. The
refusal had come from their mother, who, earlier that year, received an official request from
Dominic for a meeting about Princess Alessia.
Knowing exactly what the meeting would be
about, she'd diplomatically refused. Like the rest
of the Berrutis, the Queen abhorred the King of
Monte Cleure. Not only would she never take it
on herself to arrange her children's marriages,
she would rather lose her throne than sanction
her daughter's marriage to a man who had abso-
lute power in his principality and treated women
as playthings and those of his family as sec-
ond-class citizens. There had been many un-
confirmed rumours that he used to hit his own
sister before she fled to America.

If Clara was speaking the truth, and judging from the blunt, unfiltered way she spoke
he had no reason to doubt her, her brother had

sold her to that very man. He didn't know what was more disturbing—the idea that a man could treat his own sister in such a cruel manner or the way she relayed it so matter-of-factly and then moved straight on to another subject as if her brother selling her wasn't something that needed to be dwelt on.

'Anyway, you didn't answer my question,' she said, cutting through his disturbed thoughts. 'Do you have a girlfriend?'

He rubbed the back of his neck. 'Not at the moment.'

'Cool.'

'Cool?' he repeated.

She smiled brightly. 'I'm in your debt, remember?'

His mouth dropped open. How many shocks could one woman throw in such a short space of time? 'I thought you were a virgin?'

Now she pulled a face of disgust. 'Your mind! It's filthy! I was going to offer to buy you dinner as a thank you for rescuing me, not offer my body to you.'

He almost laughed with his relief. Clara might be the sexiest woman he'd ever met in his life but as soon as she'd mentioned the word 'virgin' he'd taken an automatic mental step back. 'I'm glad to hear it.'

'Good. I mean, you're a sexy man... Has anyone ever told you that?'

Taken aback at her nonchalant delivery, Marcelo could only answer honestly. 'Yes.'

Her expression turned to one of admiration. 'No false modesty, even better. But you are a very sexy man and very handsome so I thought it best to check that you don't have a girlfriend before making the offer of dinner because I would be miffed if you were my boyfriend and you went out for dinner with another woman. So what do you think about dinner? It might have to wait until I get back to the UK and can sort out my bank accounts—King Pig has my purse. Oh, and my passport. Where are we flying to?'

'Ceres.'

'Your island?'

'Yes.'

'Is there a British embassy?'

'Of course.'

'Good. Can you drop me there please? I'll need to get a new passport issued. Do you know how long that'll take?'

'I'm afraid not.'

She shrugged. 'Never mind. It'll take as long as it takes. Do you think they'll let me take Bob in with me?'

'I have no idea.'

She pouted and blew her cheeks out. 'Okay, I'm going to have to improvise. But that's okay.' She blew her cheeks again then fixed her sparkling eyes back on him. 'I'll blag it.'

'What does *blag it* mean?' Educated in England though he'd been and as fluent in the language as he was in his own tongue, *blag it* was a term he'd never heard before.

'I'll just walk in with him and see what happens.' She nodded vigorously. 'Okay, that's the plan sorted. I'll get my passport sorted, beg for help for a flight home if they can't sort my banking out on Ceres—if I ask nicely, they might let me give them an IOU, sort Bob out—does your island have animal shelters?' Her face clouded. 'Will they let me keep him there while I arrange everything to bring him home with me?'

'I'm sure arrangements can be made for Bob,' he assured her, barely keeping up with the thread of her thoughts. Her mind must work at supersonic speed, jumping from thread to thread in the time it took a mere mortal to think about one thing.

She brightened like a switched-on light. 'Brilliant. So, once I've got access to my bank account, can I take you out for dinner as a thank you?'

Let Clara take him out to dinner…? Now that was a decision that did not come easily. On the one hand she was ravishing and sexy and, he had to admit, entertaining. On the other hand she was a virgin. That was a big warning klaxon in his head telling him to not touch, but then it occurred to him that he was a grown man fully capable of accepting a dinner date as a means of gratitude and not as a date-date, and that sharing a meal did not have to mean the inevitability of sharing a bed afterwards.

'On one condition,' he told her.

She looked at him expectantly.

'That you occasionally give your mouth a rest and my ears a break.'

She beamed. 'Deal.'

The first Clara knew that they'd reached their destination after what felt like hours flying over the Mediterranean was when the helicopter made its descent. They'd made one refuelling stop in which she'd given Bob a quick walk—Marcelo made a makeshift lead for him—and borrowed Marcelo's phone to call her colleague Liza in England who was looking after Samson and Delilah for her and make sure they were okay and reassure Liza that she wasn't dead and would be home soon to take them off her hands.

Holding onto Bob tightly, she jumped out. They'd landed in a field, the grass of which was a bit scratchy under her bare feet, but she wasn't going to complain. Rather scratchy feet than be married to King Pig! And the sun was hot and shining on her, which was nice. It felt like an age had passed since she'd last been out in the sun, and she spent a moment enjoying the warm rays on her face.

'Right, which way's the embassy?' she asked Marcelo after she'd profusely thanked his men and pilots for rescuing her.

A look of bemusement came over his handsome face. 'You're planning to walk?'

'I'm very fit. I walk with the dogs for miles every day at home.'

He smiled. 'It's already taken care of.' He pointed to the two cars waiting by the hangar. 'The second one will take you to the embassy.'

'Oh, you are fabulous, thank you.'

'You're welcome.'

Practically bouncing on her toes to reach his face, she planted a kiss on his cheek. The bristles were soft!

Allowing herself one final stare at the gorgeous face and fabulous ice-blue eyes, Clara debated whether or not to plant a kiss to his firm mouth, just to see what that felt like too, but decided against it. She didn't want him getting the wrong idea and thinking she'd changed her mind about offering her body to him.

Instead, she reached for his hand—oh, wow, it was huge compared to hers—and squeezed the fingers. 'I know I'm going to take you out to dinner once I've sorted the mess that is my life out, but I also know it in no way repays the debt I owe you. You can call it in any time or any place and I will fulfil it. I'm not exaggerating to say you've saved my life, and probably Bob's too.'

The lines around his eyes crinkled and he squeezed her fingers in return. 'It has been... an experience.'

She cackled with laughter, knowing exactly what he meant. Clara was well aware she'd been born without a filter but situations of heightened emotions always made her motormouth tendencies worse. She thought Marcelo had done very well not to at least threaten to gag her, so kudos to him.

'It certainly has,' she agreed. 'Thanks again.'

Flipping a final wave at him, she set off to the cars, keeping her focus on the one he'd designated as hers to stop herself from looking back at him.

She'd never wanted to look back at a man before. Another first.

This really was a day of firsts. She supposed it was because Marcelo was so ruddy attractive. If she was a girl who enjoyed sexual pleasure she would have had no hesitation in offering herself to him, but Clara preferred sensory pleasure of a more inanimate kind. Beautiful clothes and stylish furniture—even second-hand ones like she had—couldn't hurt you or lie to you or abuse your trust the way humans did. Lies really were the worst because it was lies that destroyed trust. Too many, especially when they came from the very people you were programmed by birth to trust, destroyed something fundamental inside you, making it impossible to believe in anyone. The only person who'd never abused Clara's trust was her mother.

Marcelo watched her walk away, as bedraggled, truculent and sexy a sight as he had ever seen even from the rear. Even Clara's walk was sexy. She wasn't trying to be sexy. She just was.

Look at those legs. Smears of grime from the helicopter streaked her calves, scraps of what had started the day as a beautiful and expensive wedding dress clung to the toned golden thighs. Her feet were bare, long untamed hair strewn...

'Wait,' he called.

She stopped walking and turned around.

Damn it. He couldn't let her walk into the embassy like that. Sure, they would help her but there was something so wonderfully uncaring about the way she carried her dishevelment that his heart twisted on itself.

Why didn't she care?

'Come back to my place,' he said before he could change his mind. 'Have a shower and some food. I'll get Alessia to bring some clothes for you...and then I'll take you to the embassy.'

Clara's lips swirled while her eyes narrowed with thought. Then her features loosened and she grinned. 'Do you promise not to lock me in a room and threaten to kill my dog if I don't marry you? Because I'm very keen to get home to my English dogs and my job.'

Marcelo laughed at the very idea. He had nothing against marriage. He would marry one day, but not for a long time. Civilian life was so unutterably boring that the thought of settling down any time soon and losing the only excitement to be found in this royal life was, for the moment, anathema. Mind-numbing tedium was his life. The agreement with his family when he joined the army was that once his military life was over, he'd become a working member of the Berruti royal family. That his military life had come to a premature end was irrelevant. The deal stood. The adventures he'd enjoyed in his army days were memories that would have to sustain his impulsive, thrill-seeking tendencies for the rest of his life because royal life consisted of duty and decorum.

It was a shame, he mused, that Clara was a virgin, and a proud one at that. If she wasn't, he'd have no hesitation in taking the seduction path with her. A very short-lived seduction. Never minding his aversion to settling down, he had a strong feeling that wherever Clara went, chaos followed. If there was one thing incompatible with royal life, it was chaos.

She was the least virginal woman he'd ever met. In fairness, he didn't think he'd known any virgins since his school days, unless he counted his sister, who he assumed was a virgin considering she never dated, but he would rather swim in an algae-ridden pool than bring the subject up and find out. It brought him out in hives just to think it. To his mind, virgins were decorous and shy. He doubted Clara had a shy bone in her delicious body.

And she *was* delicious. There was not an inch of that body he wasn't attracted to. He could still feel the softness of her plump mouth on his cheek and the pad of his finger from when he'd pressed against it to quieten her. His finger had sunk into it.

She was hot and delicious and the least virginal of virgins in the history of virgins. A conundrum to be figured out by a better, more patient man than him.

Or a woman? Was that why she was a virgin? Did she prefer her own sex?

But he'd seen interest in her eyes. He was certain of it. Marcelo knew when a woman was attracted to him and Clara didn't have the guile to try to hide it.

But that didn't mean anything. She'd blatantly told him he was handsome and sexy. She'd also told him she had no intention of sharing her body with him and there had been nothing in those honest brown eyes to contradict that.

But as the good lady herself would say, this was all moot. He'd feed her and give her the privacy to clean herself up, and then he would send her off to the embassy and never think of her again.

Folding his arms across his chest, he raised a brow. 'I promise.'

She gambolled back to him like a spring lamb. 'Then I accept. I'm starving!'

CHAPTER THREE

'THIS IS LIKE something from a fairy tale,' Clara enthused. She opened the window and stuck her face out so she could see more clearly the ancient amphitheatre nestled alongside the castle perched high in the rolling Ceres hills. As the car rounded a bend, she saw the amphitheatre separated the castle into two distinct complex stone buildings that were a mishmash of shapes and architecture that was impressively theatrical. Here was classic medieval and renaissance and surrealist architecture blended into something fantastical, and it was huge, both the castle and the grounds. 'And I thought the house I grew up in was big! Has your family always lived here?'

'For five hundred years,' Marcelo answered.

'I bet you had some amazing games of hide-and-seek.'

'I've never played.'

The car came to a stop as she twisted to face

him. 'Really? Is that because your family is all royal and stuffy?'

His lips twitched. 'Not at all. We just played different games when I was a child.'

She nudged him with her elbow. 'Alessia invited me here for the Easter holidays once but I got expelled before it could happen and my brother wouldn't let me come as punishment. I would have got you all playing hide-and-seek.'

Her door was opened and she jumped out, already itching to explore the place. It would take weeks to explore it all. Months! Bob was just as enamoured, racing in big circles around the lawn that edged the section of the castle they were parked in front of.

Marcelo joined her. 'I never knew that.'

'What?'

'That you were going to stay with us.'

'Stay with Alessia,' she corrected, then added kindly, 'But I'm sure we would have let you play with us. But probably not your brother—Alessia said he was a right bossy-boots.'

'I would suggest you don't mention that to him,' he advised drily.

'I doubt I'll be here long enough to meet him but if I do…' She mimed zipping her lips.

The wide, full lips pulled into a grin. 'Come on, Clara Chaos, let's get some food inside you.'

Marcelo couldn't stop himself from soaking Clara's reaction to the castle interior. From the private reception room they entered and all the way down the wide corridor that led to his private quarters, her head craned this way and that, and she kept stopping to admire the artwork and, in some cases, pull a face of distaste.

When they reached his door, he unlocked it and indicated for her to enter.

'Whoa…' Her eyes were bright as she did a full circle to take everything in. 'This is yours?'

'My private quarters, yes.'

'Has it always been yours?'

'No, I lived with my siblings in my parents' quarters until I joined the army. These quarters were given to me when I turned twenty-one to use as a base when I was on leave.'

She grinned knowingly. 'Was that so you could bring women back and guarantee some privacy?'

Her cheery bluntness took him aback again.

'I bet women have always chased after you,' she said, kneeling to put Bob on the floor. Marcelo tried not to wince to see the puppy immediately roll over the thousand-year-old Persian rug.

'Haven't they?'

Not realising her comment had required an answer, Marcelo found himself at a loss at what to say. Clara was just too disarming in both her physical presence and her unnerving habit of uttering whatever came into her head.

In the end she gave a nonchalant shrug.

'You're a prince, you're rich and you're handsome. Stands to reason women would chase after you.' There was a slight narrowing of her eyes. 'But I bet you're a man who prefers to do the chasing himself. Do you ever pretend to be a commoner?'

'For what purpose?'

'To see if they still want you without all the trappings. I would. I mean, let's face it, King Pig only wanted me for my blood—that the future King of England is something like my thirteenth cousin apparently makes me a catch. And I'm poor! Anyway, is it okay for me to take a shower? I feel really grubby.'

Feeling like he'd just let a tornado into his quarters, Marcelo led her up the stairs to his guest room, which had its own bathroom attached to it. 'Help yourself to whatever you need,' he said. 'I'll get Alessia to drop some clothes over and get the chef to rustle something up for you to eat. Any dietary requirements?'

'I hate broad beans if that counts?'

'I will be sure to tell Chef that. Enjoy your shower, or you can have a bath if you prefer.' An image flashed in his mind of her reclining naked in the bath. He pushed it firmly aside and added, 'Please, take your time. There is no rush.'

She beamed. 'Thank you. Can you make sure Bob gets something to eat soon? He's only got a small belly and needs to be fed regularly.'

'I remember,' he assured her. At their earlier fuel stop Clara had managed to charm—or, more likely, bamboozle—one of the pilots into giving up his beef sandwich so she could feed it in small chunks to the puppy. She hadn't taken a scrap of it for herself. 'I will sort it as a priority.'

'You are clearly taking the path straight to heaven, thank you.'

Still smiling, she closed the bathroom door. The distinct sound of it locking echoed through the oak.

Marcelo gazed down at the fluffball at his feet and sighed before lifting him into his arms. 'I don't know about you, Bob,' he said in his native tongue, 'but your owner is a unique force of nature.'

Bob licked his face in agreement.

This was one amazing bathroom in one amazing set of private quarters in one amazing castle. The House of Fernandez's palace in Monte Cleure was beautiful too and comparable in size, but the Berruti castle had character and intrigue seeped in its walls. Well, the walls she'd seen, which was only a teeny fraction of it all.

Soaking in the huge roll-top tub, Clara happily admired the frescoed ceiling high above her featuring naked cherubs and nymphs splashing and swimming in a natural pool in the middle of a wood. Very sensual. Very fitting for the man it belonged to. If this was Marcelo's guest bathroom, what kind of bathroom did he have for his own private use? If the rest of his private quarters were an indication, she'd guess something akin to a Roman bath.

When boredom kicked in, she washed her hair, scrubbed her body, grabbed the towel closest to hand and climbed out.

Marcelo's guest bathroom came equipped with a full array of toiletries and after drying herself, she brushed her teeth with a new brush but was disappointed not to find any cosmetics. Clara loved wearing make-up, felt naked without it. Maybe Alessia would let her borrow some. She looked forward to seeing her old friend. Alessia had been the only girl at their horrible boarding school Clara had liked.

Securing the towel around herself, she stepped into the adjoining room. It matched her prison cell for size and had the requisite four-poster bed, but it had far more personality and the most fabulous pale blue satin sofa that wasn't really a sofa, more a four-bottoms-wide padded chair with gold legs and arms. Plus, if she found herself imprisoned in it, she was only one floor off the ground and could easily jump to safety.

'Marcelo?' she called as she left the room. When there was no answer, she wandered down the stairs and into the living room. As she called his name a second time, French doors opened and he stepped in from his private garden with Bob at his heels.

'There you are,' she said, kneeling to scoop up Bob, who'd come tearing over to her. 'Did you manage to get any clean clothes for me?'

From the look of his damp hair and the fresh scent emanating from him, Clara guessed Marcelo had showered. He'd changed out of the tuxedo into a pair of tight-fitting blue jeans and white V-necked T-shirt that admirably displayed his sexy, muscular physique. Oh, he looked *good*. And that scent!

He turned his head away from her and spoke through what were clearly clenched teeth. 'I put them on the guest bed for you. Didn't you hear me call out to you?'

'No. You should have shouted. Is something the matter?'

'No.'

'Are you sure? You seem very tense.'

His chest rose. The square jaw was definitely locked. 'Alessia isn't in so I've given you some of my own clothes to wear.'

'Ha! You're twice the size of me.'

'They're clean. Go and get changed.'

'Okay... You sure you're okay?'

He inclined his head curtly, still not looking at her. 'Food will be ready in a few minutes.'

'Cool.' She stepped to him, ready to hand the

puppy over if the answer to her question was no.
'Is Bob allowed upstairs with me?'

'No… Yes. That's fine.'

Marcelo held his breath until she'd left the room and he heard her footsteps bounding up the stairs.

Sinking into the nearest chair, he pressed the palm of his hand to his forehead and tried to rid himself of the image of Clara dressed in nothing but a tiny towel. It was not a sight he'd been expecting and the effect had been immediate and potent. He'd had to hold his breath to stop the warm scent of freshly bathed Clara from dousing his senses and avert his eyes from the feast that was her knockout body wrapped in nothing but a small towel.

His evasions hadn't been quick enough. Both her scent and the image had burned into him. *Dio*, his heart was still thumping. His loins still throbbed.

She had been oblivious to the effect. If any other woman had paraded before him in a tiny towel he'd have assumed it was deliberate, but Clara had acted as if it were perfectly normal.

Couldn't she have wrapped herself in one of the oversized towels? Did she have to select one that barely skimmed her buttocks?

He took some long breaths and reminded himself that in an hour or so he'd be able to send Clara to the embassy with his conscience clear. He'd make a call on her behalf, he decided. Smooth her path. He was a prince of the country, his word held sway. He'd put all his resources at Clara's and the embassy's disposal. Anything to get this dangerously sexy but untouchable woman off his island and allow his equilibrium to return to its normal state.

But then she joined him in the dining room and his heart thumped hard again.

'I need your help,' she said, and lifted the navy polo shirt he'd given her to her waist. The belt he'd provided her with to hold his jeans up was too big even fastened at the tightest notch. 'These are going to fall down. Can you make another hole in the belt for me? I don't mind if you'd rather not ruin it doing that as the polo shirt is long enough for me to wear as a dress, but I haven't got any knickers on and if there's a gust of wind when I leave the castle I might frighten your fellow countrymen.'

He gritted his teeth to fight off the imagery and beckoned the nearest servant to fetch him a sharp, pointed knife.

'Take the belt off,' he said in a curter tone than intended.

'Okay.' She pulled it off and, as she passed it to him, the jeans fell to her ankles. Stepping out of them, she picked them up and put them on the back of the chair next to hers and took her seat. 'What's for dinner?'

He filled his lungs with much needed air before answering. 'Roast mushroom gnocchi.'

'It smells wonderful.'

Their bowls were filled for them and a knife for Marcelo to make a notch in the belt placed beside him.

'You've got that face again,' Clara observed after barely a minute of silence while they ate.

'What face?'

'*That* face. All tense, like you're sucking on a particularly sour lemon. Don't you like gnocchi?'

She was observant. That supersonic brain didn't miss anything.

How would she respond if he imitated her unfiltered bluntness and said, *If I'm tense, it's because you're the sexiest creature I've ever met and you've candidly declared that you're not wearing any knickers and I can clearly see you're not wearing a bra either and right now I can't stop my mind from imagining you naked and my taste buds are salivating to imagine the taste of your skin, and I feel as horny as the horniest of teenagers.*

'I have a headache,' he answered, hoping she would take the hint and keep quiet for a little longer.

It wasn't what she said that made him wish for her silence, he recognised. It was her voice. The more he listened to it, the more he wanted to listen. It had a musicality that was as alluring and entertaining as the rest of her.

Clara Sinclair aroused *all* his senses. And more.

'Have you taken any painkillers?' she asked.

'Not yet.'

She managed another minute of silence before piping up with, 'I put my dirty clothes in the laundry basket but if you get me a bag, I'll bin them. Unless you have an incinerator?'

He shook his head and helped himself to more parmesan. He didn't trust himself to look at her, not when his eyes itched to study her like a rare masterpiece. Many women stripped of their make-up looked washed out. Not Clara. Her natural luminosity shone through and elevated her beauty.

When Marcelo had been a child, his father would drag him around the castle trying to pique his interest in the thousands of pieces of art in the royal collection. Occasionally—very occasionally—a painting or sculpture would capture his interest and then he would be captivated enough to return to it time and time again. Those particular items were now housed here in his private quarters.

He wanted to stare at Clara as he still often gazed at those masterpieces.

As soon as he finished eating, Marcelo set to

work on the belt. Once he'd stabbed the hole in it, he handed it back to her.

Smiling her thanks, she snatched her jeans off the chair beside her, threaded the belt through then stuck her legs in them and hopped onto her feet. Twisting around so her back was to him, she pulled them up her thighs. Unprepared for the glimpse of peachy buttock as the denim was pulled over her bottom, Marcelo was unable to stop himself from snapping, 'Do you not have *any* modesty?'

She spun around. Startled brown eyes fixed on him. 'What are you talking about?'

He gritted his teeth. He didn't know whether to laugh or shout at her blitheness. 'I just saw your bottom.'

And coming so soon after she'd nonchalantly walked around in front of him in a teeny towel, an image he'd been doing his damned best to scrub from his retinas, had the effect of adding fuel to the fire he'd only just brought down to a moderate simmer.

She fastened the belt. 'So? It's only flesh. We all have it.'

Yes, but not everyone's flesh is as delectable as yours.

'Did you parade in front of Dominic in a towel?' he asked tautly, not because he thought she would have done but to make a point.

Plonking herself back on her seat, she inched

the chair back and began rolling the jeans up at the ankles. 'Dominic gave me the heebie-jeebies from the word go. You don't.'

'I'm still a man, Clara.'

'And?'

'You're a beautiful woman,' he told her stiffly. A very beautiful, incredibly sexy woman. A woman who, if she wasn't a virgin, he would seduce without a second thought.

'And?'

'I see you don't suffer from false modesty either.'

'I can't help how I look any more than you can help how you look,' she said with her usual bluntness.

He took hold of his glass of water and held it tightly as he brought it to his lips. 'It doesn't bother you, parading around half-naked in a towel and allowing a glimpse of your backside to a man?' Surely she must see the danger?

'I wasn't parading and I didn't allow you a glimpse. I turned my back to you so you wouldn't be embarrassed about seeing my vagina.'

He almost choked on the water he was about to swallow.

She covered her mouth, clearly suppressing a giggle. 'I would never have pegged you as prudish.'

That annoyed him. 'I am not prudish.'

'Then why are you acting prudish? I thought you'd seen plenty of female flesh in your adult life?'

'There is a time and a place.'

'We're in your private quarters. Who else is going to see me?' she asked with infuriating reasonableness.

'That is not the point.'

'But it's *my* point.'

'You're not worried I might be overtaken by lust?'

'Why? Are you?'

'Of course not.'

'Then what's your problem?'

The woman could turn a saint to drink. 'Your lack of self-preservation!'

She swirled her lips, a groove appearing on her forehead. 'It's very touching that you care but you don't need to worry about me. To me, human flesh is just flesh, the wrapping of the human body, but if you're worried about your own control then don't—if I thought you were in any way a monster, I wouldn't be sitting here, and if it makes you feel better, I've been taking self-defence classes for years.'

Spotting the contradiction in this, he said, 'Because of the threat men pose to you?'

But she dismissed his assumption with a, 'No, because of the threat they pose to my dogs.'

He was incredulous. 'Your dogs?'

'Dognapping has become increasingly common and I'm not going to let anyone take mine from me without a fight.' The serious hue of her eyes turned into a sparkle. 'I can show you my moves if you want?'

Now he'd heard everything. 'You think you could *fight* me?'

Her eyebrows waggled with mischief. 'Wanna try?'

'No!'

'Is that because you're so much bigger than me and think you would hurt me? Because I assure you, it's far more likely that I would hurt you.'

Surely she couldn't believe that, he thought incredulously. He was big enough and strong enough to snap her in two. 'Would you have been able to fight Dominic off when he tried to force himself on you?' he challenged. It was a challenge that sent nausea roiling violently in his stomach as, for the first time, he realised what the implications would have been if he hadn't rescued her that morning.

The sparkle faded to nothing and he knew Clara was thinking the exact same thing.

'I was prepared to,' she said, speaking quietly for the first time. 'I would have fought like hell. I tried to fight him when he first locked me up but he had his bodyguards flanking him and they stopped me. He always had them at his side when he dealt with me.'

Bile rose up his throat. 'Did he hurt you when he dealt with you?'

She shook her head and gave her first bitter smile. 'He didn't want my skin marred for the wedding photos.'

The bile flooded his mouth. It was the most rancid taste he'd ever experienced and, for the first time in his life, Marcelo wished to harm someone. Properly harm them. Maim them.

Before he could swallow the foul taste, his private secretary tapped on the door and slipped into the room.

What she whispered in his ear made his stomach pitch.

Maintaining his composure, he rose to his feet. 'Excuse me,' he said to Clara. 'My mother has requested a meeting with me. Have some dessert. I shouldn't be long.'

And then, on his return, he would see her into a car and wave goodbye to the sexiest, most infuriating woman he'd ever met in his life.

'You cannot be serious?'

The looks on the faces of Marcelo's parents and siblings on the other side of the table, all convened for this family emergency, told him they were.

He kneaded his temples in an effort to temper the forming headache. 'I can't marry her. Dear God, Clara Sinclair is completely unsuited to being a member of *any* royal family let alone this one.'

'Dominic thought she was good enough for him,' his mother pointed out.

'Dominic was, by Clara's own admission, desperate.'

'Our situation will become desperate if you don't,' Amadeo, his brother, said. 'As Mother said, it doesn't have to be for ever, only a year or two, just long enough to be convincing.'

'Even a day is too long. She has no decorum and no filter on her mouth.'

'Then you will have to teach her.'

'I am not a miracle worker.'

His mother put her hand flat on the table and leaned forward. 'What matters is the public's perception. This has the potential to destroy us. Marrying her is the only way to mitigate the trouble your actions, however noble they were, have brought on this family.'

Marcelo looked from face to face. Beneath the implacable facades lay compassion. They all knew he wasn't ready to marry.

But they knew—and he knew—that this mess was a situation of his own making and that it was his responsibility to fix it before the snow-ball he'd set off turned into an avalanche.

He threw his hands in the air. 'Okay, I'll ask her, but she won't agree to it. Clara doesn't want to get married. She wants to get back to England and resume her life.'

'Then it's up to you to convince her,' his father said. 'For all our sakes.'

CHAPTER FOUR

FOR WANT OF something to do in Marcelo's absence, Clara decided to clear the table, but no sooner had she started when two members of his staff bustled in and insisted she leave it to them.

Was there anything worse than boredom? she wondered. She'd been bored rigid in her Monte Cleure prison cell but at least she'd successfully kept her mind occupied thinking of escape routes and ways to torture Dominic, and dreaming up insults and cutting remarks to her women gaolers who so rarely left her side.

She had no idea why it had upset her when Marcelo challenged her about whether she'd have been able to fight Dominic off. It had got to the stage where she believed rescue would never come so she'd made her plans for it, and those plans were simply to fight until her last breath. It had amused her to imagine the public's reaction to her wedding night death. Better than the alternative of imagining her own corpse. The thought of her own death as a concept didn't particularly bother her. So long as her animals back home were taken care of then she was happy to go. It wasn't that she didn't enjoy life—she did, very much, even if at times it felt a little lonely—but more that she didn't fear the pain and grief for those she loved, mainly because there wasn't anyone left who loved her. It was a simple fact. She thought some of her colleagues might miss her, some might even shed a tear, but they wouldn't *grieve* her and would probably quickly forget her. Even Samson and Delilah, her dogs, would transfer their affection to Liza. Dogs lived in the moment. It was an ethos Clara tried hard to emulate.

Maybe Marcelo's challenge had upset her because she'd had a fleeting moment of wondering what if? As in, what if Marcelo hadn't rescued her?

Clara didn't deal with what ifs. They were pointless. When bad stuff happened the only way forward was to dust yourself down, put it behind you and carry on.

How funny, though, that he should be so prudish about flesh. It hadn't occurred to her that he'd be uncomfortable to see her in a towel. Marcelo had had lots of lovers.

She remembered catching a glimpse of him when she was fifteen and he'd turned up at her boarding school one Saturday to take Alessia out. Clara had been confined to her room that weekend for some misdemeanour or other, and she'd sat on her windowsill watching the bustle of activity unfolding in the grounds when the tall, gorgeous stranger had caught her eye. She'd guessed by Alessia's reaction that he was one of her brothers and when she'd been subsequently put in a room with the Ceresian princess some months later, she'd asked about him. And that had been that. Clara hadn't given him another thought in the following years, apart from the times when she flicked through social media and caught a glimpse of his name. She always followed the links, always hoping to find he'd settled down with one of the beautiful women he was often pictured with. Any man who went out of his way to take his little sister on jollies from boarding school was all right in Clara's book and deserved to find happiness. Andrew hadn't made a single visit in all her years there.

She supposed that's why it hadn't occurred to her that her flesh would make Marcelo uncomfortable because, to a degree, she trusted him so it hadn't occurred to her that it would be more appropriate—how she *hated* that word. She'd lost count of the times her teachers would say, 'That is not appropriate behaviour, Miss Sinclair.'—to leave the room before putting the jeans back on. The towel couldn't be helped as she genuinely hadn't seen the clothes on the bed, but even if she had, the same degree of trust in

Marcelo applied. He would not lay an unwanted finger on her.

Trust, however limited, in a man? In *any* human? This really was a day of firsts.

Helping herself to a slice of the lemon mousse brought in for her, she stretched her legs out and wriggled her bare toes and contemplated that it was just as well she'd be leaving for the embassy soon. Marcelo made her feel all funny inside. More nervous energy than usual ran through her veins and she kept staring at the dining room door like she was waiting with bated breath for his return. This was curious and a touch disconcerting. But only a touch. Lots of women, she imagined, would have a fit of the vapours to be in his presence so in comparison the effect he had on her was minor.

All the same, she found herself straightening when he returned to the dining room.

He closed the door behind him.

One look at his face told her something terrible had happened.

She half rose from her chair. 'Has someone died?'

A look of amused but pained torture contorted his gorgeous features, and he shook his head, lowering himself into his seat and gripping at his hair.

He closed his eyes for a long moment and,

when he opened them, fixed them directly on her. 'There is no easy way to say this.'

'Then just say it,' she encouraged. 'Straight to the point is always best.'

The corners of his lips twitched for a moment before his shoulders rose and he took a deep breath. 'I need to convince you to marry me.'

Marcelo watched Clara carefully, bracing himself for whatever unpredictable reaction she would give.

The large eyes widened. The plump mouth sucked in so hard her cheeks sucked in with them, disappearing until her lips were the size and shape of a bird's beak.

And then she covered the bird's beak and half her face with her hand, and her shoulders began to shake. To his alarm, tears spilled over the hand smothering her mouth but the alarm barely had time to register for she whipped the hand away, slapped it on the table and threw her head back.

She wasn't crying. She was laughing. She was convulsed with it.

She slapped the table a number of times and must have swiped at the tears a dozen times before she regained control of herself, and even then her chest and shoulders continued to shake.

'Marry you?' she finally managed to splutter. 'I've heard everything now. And you're *serious*!' More laughter echoed around the room. 'You *are*. I can see it on your face. You want me to marry you! Is that what your mother wanted to see you for? Is this her idea? No way it's yours. She must be desperate!'

Marcelo had left his family feeling as if he had the weight of the entire castle on his shoulders, but now, with Clara's laughter ringing in his ears and her glee shining before his eyes, he felt that weight lift.

He'd imagined tantrums. He'd imagined her throwing things at him. He'd imagined curses. He'd imagined her making a running jump through one of the dining room windows and then continuing to run until she found the British embassy.

Knowing she preferred straight to the point honesty, he said, 'Yes. Unfortunately my rescuing you did not go undetected—your guards broke the door down and managed to get some pictures of us hanging from the helicopter. Dominic has launched a full diplomatic war and is making threats against our nation. To get public and political opinion on our side, not just here on Ceres but in Europe, my mother and the rest of my family think we should marry as soon as possible and spin things that you and I are a love match and that I stole you away from Dominic because I had been a stubborn fool who didn't realise until it was nearly too late how much I love you and couldn't bear to see you married to someone else.'

'That's what your family thinks?' There was a flash of astuteness. 'And what do *you* think?'

He sighed and pushed his chair back. Rising to his feet, he said, 'I think I need a drink. Want one?'

She stretched her legs out, hooked her ankles together and folded her arms across her ample breasts. 'Why not?'

He removed a full bottle of fifteen-year-old Scotch and two glasses from the cabinet at the far end of the room and carried them to the table. Pouring them both a hefty measure, he slid one to Clara and took a large drink from the other.

He let the welcome fire burn down his throat and said, 'I'm afraid that I agree with my family.'

Once his mother had spelled out how quickly and spectacularly the fallout of his rescue had spread, there had been no other conclusion to reach.

It was his mother's disappointment that smarted the most. That it was deserved disappointment only made it worse.

Marcelo had let his ego and need for excitement overrule his good sense, and now Dominic had a clear photograph of Marcelo's face as he held tightly to Clara in her wedding dress hanging from a helicopter flying above the House of Fernandez palace. Marcelo was media savvy enough to know it was going to be press dynamite.

His family were right to be angry with him. He was furious with himself. Three years of duty and self-control thrown away in one impulsive action causing a diplomatic incident that could easily escalate. Unlike Ceres, which had a ruling government, Monte Cleure had a ruling monarchy, which meant Dominic was in charge. The Berruti royal family were mere figureheads of their great nation, an anachronistic relic of the past kept alive only because of the affection of its people. It had been drilled into Marcelo and his siblings since they first learned to talk how precarious their positions and titles were. Their castle was wholly owned by the family, its upkeep and maintenance paid for by the income from foreign tourists—they allowed Ceresians in for free—but everything else that came with their position was subject to keeping the public and politicians onside.

Ceres people were romantics at heart. They would forgive a tale of madness caused by love more easily than they would a tale of madness caused by ego, boredom and a loss of self-control.

'Have you got a copy of the photo of us?' she asked once she'd had a sip of her Scotch.

'On my phone.' He brought up the picture that had been forwarded to him and passed it to her.

She studied it with avid interest. 'You can't see my face to identify me but that's definitely you.'

The guard who'd taken the photo had captured Marcelo's face in its entirety.

'When I manage to get a new phone you'll have to send it to me,' she added, pushing the phone back to him. 'I might get it made into a poster and stick it on my bedroom wall…although I might have to photoshop my bum—it looks huge!'

If he wasn't so filled with anger at himself and the dangerous situation he'd put his family in, he would have laughed.

'If I refuse to marry you, what happens?' she asked. 'Do you lock me in a room and put armed guards outside my door to stop me escaping, then drag me up the aisle and threaten to kill my dog if I make a scene?'

Marcelo raised an incredulous eyebrow that she even had to ask that, then had another drink of his Scotch and rubbed his forehead. 'I can't force you to marry me. My family have much influence in this country but our power is limited. And if I could force you to marry me, I wouldn't—I didn't rescue you from that bastard to force you into an unwanted life with me.'

Curiosity danced in her eyes. 'Then why did you?'

'Boredom.'

'Boredom?'

Marcelo grunted and shook his head in self-recrimination. That's what his actions boiled down to. Boredom. Three years of unswerving, mind-numbing tedium dressed as duty had been smashed apart by one loss of tightly leashed self-control.

He must never let it happen again.

A slow grin spread over Clara's face. 'If I marry you, I guarantee you won't be bored.'

That pulled him up, and he studied her open face. 'You're not considering it?'

The grin didn't dim a jot as she downed her drink and pushed the glass back to him. 'Fill me up, big boy. And yourself. My demands don't come cheap.'

He couldn't believe she was even contemplating it. 'You are serious?'

'I'm in your debt, remember? I mean, you can't have forgotten. You only rescued me, what, ten hours ago?'

Was that all the time that had passed?

He refilled her glass. 'Marrying me goes far beyond any debt you owe me.'

'Not to my mind. You saved my life and Bob's life. I'm happy to be a princess for a while if you're certain it will help...' Her eyes narrowed slightly. 'We wouldn't have to share a bed, would we?'

'*No.*' His answer was emphatic but her question made him reel as sleeping arrangements were something he hadn't yet considered. There hadn't been time to consider anything other than his mother's forceful if sympathetic insistence that he fix the mess he'd created for their family and their people by marrying Clara.

'And we wouldn't be expected to stay married for ever, would we?' she asked before he could consider the other implications of marriage to this truculently sexy, wholly unsuitable creature.

But his body was already considering it, a tightening in his loins...

'I mean, would we be allowed to divorce?' she continued. 'It wouldn't bother me if we didn't but I assume you want to settle down in a real marriage at some point? By the way, are you okay? You've gone all face-sucking lemons again.'

Realising his fists were clenched, Marcelo loosened them and tried to loosen his jaw too. Clara didn't miss a trick and, unlike him, didn't need time to consider things, her supersonic brain taking everything in and digesting it and moving straight to the tangents and implications of each one.

'Divorce is allowed here after two years of marriage,' he said. 'We would have to put on a show of being together for, say, a year, and then quietly go our separate ways—'

'We can let people believe I'm homesick for

England!' she interrupted enthusiastically, his answer clearly having put her mind at ease.

'That would work, I'm sure, and then after a year of quiet separation, file for divorce.'

'Cool.'

'Cool?' he echoed in disbelief.

'It all sounds very reasonable. But I do have demands…well, requests. I'll marry you whether you agree to them or not.'

'Name them.'

She held her hand up and, as she listed her requests, ticked them off with her fingers. 'I want Samson and Delilah brought over to live here, preferably by car. And clothes. Lots of beautiful clothes. And cosmetics. The good stuff.' The good stuff like her mum used to have. Clara's memories of her mum had faded over time but the scent of expensive make-up could evoke her face as clearly as if she was standing right in front of her. It would evoke too the beautiful clothes her mother had worn with such panache. Much better to remember her looking and smelling wonderful than to remember how she'd been at the end. 'And I would like a donation made to the animal sanctuary I work at to cover all their costs for the next five years and a decent lump sum paid to my colleague Liza—she's the one I called earlier who's been looking after Samson and Delilah for me.'

'What else?'

'If it's not too selfish a request, when we separate, can you buy me a house in the English countryside? Nothing too big, two bedrooms will be ample, a big one for me and my dogs, and one for my clothes. And I would like a bit of land so I can open my own animal sanctuary. So maybe a house with an outbuilding?'

'Anything else?'

She thought hard before giving a decisive shake of her head. 'No. That's everything.'

If Marcelo's incredulity pulled any tighter it would snap. 'Do you know how much my family is worth?'

Her shoulders rose in a don't-care shrug.

'Billions.' Along with the castle that was their main home, the Berruti royal family had a portfolio of assets spread across their own island, neighbouring Sicily and mainland Italy that had been owned by them for centuries. Acutely aware that, though loved by their public, Ceresian society had evolved and that they could no longer justify any of their lifestyle being funded from the public purse, beginning with his grandfather, the family had actively monetised those assets and cannily added to them, and paid a crack team of people to run it all for them under the family's supervision. All that and the royal art collection too.

Not a flicker of being impressed crossed

Clara's face. If anything, there was a flicker of distaste there.

'Money doesn't interest you?'

'I only care that I have enough of it to live on. Money turns people into monsters,' she replied in as flat a tone as he'd heard from those lips before.

'My family are not monsters.' If they'd been monsters he wouldn't feel so rotten for imperilling them with his rash actions.

The grin returned. 'I know that. Maybe your family are the exceptions? I take it you've warned them what a nightmare I am and how utterly unsuited I am for the role of a princess?'

His mouth dropped open. Not only did she have a supersonic brain but she was a mind reader as well.

She sniggered and drank more of her Scotch. 'I'll take that as a yes. Doesn't that just prove how desperate King Pig was for a wife? You might need to gag me when we're out in public though. So, when are we getting married?'

Marcelo rubbed his aching head. 'You are sure you agree to this? It is a big thing I'm asking of you.'

He shouldn't be trying to talk her out of the sacrifice she was prepared to make when the alternative could mean the destruction of the Berruti royal family.

'You're not asking, I'm volunteering.' Her

shoulders rose again. This time he wasn't quick enough to avert his eyes from seeing her un-bound breasts move under the polo shirt with the motion, and he had to clench his teeth to counter the stab of lust that lanced him from it.

Dio, he needed sleep. A full eight hours would do the trick of restoring the connection between the brain in his head and the brain between his legs.

'It'll be fun,' she added.

'I can't guarantee that.' Fun was the last word he'd use to describe his life.

'I can,' she refuted brightly.

Despite everything, laughter burst out of him, and, finally accepting that this was the path he had to follow for the next year, he raised his glass. 'To a successful fake marriage.'

Eyes brimming with merriment, she clinked her glass to it. 'Long may it not continue.'

In unison, they tipped their drinks down their throats.

The deal was sealed.

God help him.

Clara tapped quietly on Marcelo's bedroom door; quietly in case he was asleep. She'd nearly fallen asleep herself when she'd remembered something and sat bolt upright.

To her relief, the handle turned and the door partially opened. Marcelo's face appeared in the gap. Straight away she saw he had no top on and found herself in the novel situation of trying to stop her stare from drifting down so she could get a good look at his naked chest.

Her eyes won and she dipped her stare to eye level and caught a glimpse of broad golden shoulders and defined pecs with a healthy smattering of dark hair whorled in the centre.

'Is something the matter?' he asked, and she quickly looked back at his face.

Probably it was having only the light from her bedroom illuminating the hallway causing it but he looked even more gorgeous than when she'd wished him a goodnight, so gorgeous that as she gazed into his eyes a warmth spread through her like a steadily creeping flush. Marcelo's voice sounded more gravelly too. Sexier. For the first time she noticed the hint of an accent in it.

'Clara? Is something the matter?' he repeated.

She cleared her throat. 'Yes,' she replied quickly, and castigated herself for being distracted by a man with no top on. How silly was that? All the same, with the faint scent of warm male now hitting her senses, she thought it prudent to step back before continuing. 'Well, it's something that matters to me. I know I said I didn't have any further requests but can I keep Bob?'

A faint smile appeared on his shadowed face. 'I assumed that was a given.'

She put her hand to her chest—Lord, her heart was thumping—and expelled her relief. 'Thank you. That's everything.' She sidestepped away from his door. 'Sorry for disturbing you.' Another sidestep nearer to her own door. 'Goodnight.'

'Goodnight, Clara.'

She threw herself back into what was no longer a guest room but *her* room and tried not to slam the door behind her in her haste.

What on earth had just happened?

What had possessed her body to act as if she'd never seen a topless man before? She'd seen plenty of naked male chests in magazines and on social media. Loads. And she was quite sure she'd seen her brother topless once, when she'd been around ten in an exceptionally hot summer, so hot that even Andrew had felt compelled to remove his stuffy tweed suit. Or she might have dreamt that last part. Dream or not, thanks to technology, the male body was no mystery to her, so why she should react in such a way was *bizarre*.

Climbing back under the sheets, she gazed at the canopy of her bed and breathed deeply. Hopefully lots of air in her lungs would settle her heartbeat. She let her arm drop over the side so Bob could nuzzle back into her hand as he liked to do before he fell asleep. She'd given him a couple of her pillows to use as a bed. Marcelo was taking her shopping tomorrow. She'd ask if he would buy Bob a proper bed.

Who'd have thought she'd end the day with a reminder to herself to ask Prince Marcelo Berruti to buy a dog bed?

What an extraordinary day it had been. She'd woken feeling sick, certain the day was going to end with her death or something worse and here she was now, sleeping in a room every bit as sumptuous as her prison cell but with the door unlocked and no fear in her heart, and that was entirely down to Marcelo. He'd saved her life and the life of her defenceless puppy. He'd put his own life on the line for her—at the time she'd been too caught in the moment to appreciate the inherent danger of his rescue—and the more she thought about it, the more her heart swelled with gratitude that a stranger would go to such lengths for her.

Deep down she hadn't believed that anyone would care enough to attempt the rescue, and she didn't care that he'd done it because, by his own admittance, he was bored. She was alone in this bed, unharmed and whole because of him, and for that she would gladly pledge a year of her life to him. He was honest too, a trait Clara valued above everything. He could have spun her a tale about wanting to rescue a damsel in distress because *it was the right thing to do* or some other such nonsense, but he'd stuck with the truth. Kudos to him. But his rescue of her and failure to see the potential fallout of his actions signified another of his personality traits—impetuousness. She guessed that must be a nature thing because ten years in the military would have taught him to use his brain as well as his brawn.

Being practically twice her height and definitely twice her width, Marcelo had a *lot* of brawn. She hoped he continued wearing white T-shirts. They looked good on him and really flattered his physique—his pecs were *amazing*, and even better, as she now knew, in the flesh. The work that must go into maintaining them! There had been a time earlier that evening when they'd been discussing how they were going to handle things over the next few weeks and she'd noticed his nipples through his T-shirt. She'd felt a mad urge to tweak one of them. What was *that* all about? Weird. Hopefully she wouldn't get too many mad urges like that in the future. Or that other weird moment when her fingers had tingled to touch the soft bristles of his stubbly beard again. Why that had happened she couldn't figure out. Her curiosity had already been sated on that score, so why want to touch it again?

When Bob left her hand to curl up on his makeshift bed, Clara lifted her now numb arm and did likewise. Burrowing under the sheets, she continued to think about Marcelo.

When sleep eventually enveloped her, Marcelo's face was the last thing her conscious mind saw.

CHAPTER FIVE

CLARA'S DELIGHT TO find Alessia in the living area when she came down the next morning was evident by the joy on her face even before she threw herself at her. 'It is so good to see you,' she enthused, embracing her tightly. 'Thank you, thank you for sending your brother to rescue me.'

'It was nothing,' Alessia laughed. 'Can you let me go now? I'm having trouble breathing.'

'Sorry.' Giggling, Clara unwound her arms but put her hands on Alessia's biceps so she could study her properly. 'You look fantastic.'

'Thank you. You're looking good too.'

'Ha! I look like I've been dragged through a hedge backwards. I haven't even brushed my hair yet.'

Marcelo watched the exchange with the strangest tightness in his chest. Clara was still wearing his polo shirt. It still fell to her knees. He was still unable to eradicate from his mind that beneath it she was naked. Hours he'd spent, lying in his bed, trying to switch his brain off, but the current running through his veins had been too strong for sleep to come easily. There had been too much running through his head too.

One impulsive act in three years had changed his life irrevocably.

If he'd stuck to the original plan, Clara would have still been rescued but his presence in the wedding chapel would have been proof of his innocence in the matter. There would be no diplomatic or trade threat to his country.

He still couldn't wrap his head around how quickly she'd agreed to marry him. She could have refused and there would have been nothing he could do about it. But she'd had no hesitation in agreeing to it. To insisting.

What kind of woman did that?

A woman like Clara Sinclair.

As short as their time together had been, it had been more than enough for him to learn a great deal about her, more than he'd ever learned about anyone in such a short time. Clara was too open for there to be any ambiguity. She didn't *do* ambiguity. She did unfiltered honesty.

She'd processed the seriousness of the situation and, feeling she owed him her life, had pledged herself to him. It had been as simple as that.

The weight of responsibility lay heavily in him. Responsibility to Clara to make the next year as easy for her as he could while she navigated her way through the royal role she was to selflessly undertake. Responsibility to his family to ensure Clara made that navigation seamlessly without further damage to the monarchy.

The pitfalls, though, were obvious. A loose cannon was marrying into his family. A loose cannon who made his blood thicken just to look at her.

The only thing that had made him take a mental step back from his desire for Clara had been her virginity. It had been an easy step to take when he'd expected to spend no more than a few hours with her.

Gazing at her now, dishevelled from sleep and as sexy a sight as he'd ever seen, he couldn't work out if it was excitement or dread thrumming through his veins at what his immediate future held.

There shouldn't *be* any thrumming. Excitement had no place in his life. Adrenaline, mad rushes of blood to the head…those were the things that drove a man to act on impulse and do foolish, thoughtless things like personally rescue a distressed damsel from a cruel king.

'Can you believe we're going to be sisters?' Clara enthused to his sister as she bounded to the French doors to let Bob into the garden. 'How crazy is that?'

'Crazy,' Alessia agreed, although she was

the only member of Marcelo's immediate family who hadn't been surprised at Clara's ready agreement to marry him, which he'd informed them about after his and Clara's talk. His parents and brother had all been dumbstruck. He was quite sure Clara would have found their expressions funny.

The amusement left Clara's face. 'But you know it isn't for ever?' she said, her tone serious.

'Marcelo explained everything.'

'Good.' The smile returned. 'It is always best to be honest. Your brother is a very sexy man but I like living on my own. I don't think I could cope if it was for ever. And I don't think Marcelo could cope with me for very long either.'

Alessia's face showed she was trying not to laugh. 'We're just grateful that you've agreed to marry him at all.'

'It's the least I can do. Just not for ever.'

Somehow her face managed to glow even brighter when Alessia showed her the dress she'd brought over from her own quarters for Clara to wear that day.

'It's a maxi-dress on me,' Alessia explained. 'But it's roomy so you should be able to fit in it okay.'

Compared to Marcelo's six-foot-three height, Clara was short. Compared to his diminutive sister who, like their mother, didn't even reach five foot and was as thin as a pencil, she was tall. Short or tall, Clara had curves in abundance, and he almost got a full view of her voluptuousness when she crossed her arms to grab the fabric of her polo shirt dress, clearly about to whip it off, but then her gaze landed on him and, after a moment's thought, stopped what she was doing.

Shooting him a cheeky look that quite clearly said, 'See, I can be modest,' she gathered Alessia's dress into her arms. 'I'll take a shower. I don't suppose you've got any make-up on you?' she added hopefully to his sister.

'Sorry. We can get you all the make-up you want when we go shopping.'

'You're coming with us?'

'Marcelo's asked me to take you.'

He was not prepared for the disappointed pout Clara threw at him. 'You're not coming?'

'No,' he said smoothly. 'There is much to organise for our wedding, and besides, Alessia will be a better shopping partner for you. I get bored easily.'

'So do I! But not when shopping for clothes. I can do that all day.' She turned back to Alessia. 'You can give me some pointers on princess stuff when we're out—I really don't want to embarrass you all once I'm thrown under the public gaze so I'll need strict instructions on how to behave.' Hardly drawing breath and not waiting for his sister to respond, she spoke again to

Marcelo. 'Will you look after Bob while we're gone?' The puppy had come in from his trip to the garden and was currently trying to scramble onto a seventeenth-century armchair.

'No problem.'

She beamed. 'I'm going to get ready. Won't be long.'

The silence Clara left in her wake was like the aftermath of a tornado.

Marcelo found himself reluctant to meet his sister's stare. When he did, she gave a rueful smile. 'She likes you.'

'I like her too.' To his own amazement, he found this was true. Clara Sinclair was a force of nature—a *handful* as Alessia had described her—and honest to the point of rudeness, but he fully understood too what Alessia had meant about her being inherently loveable.

But what he didn't like was the way he responded to her, and it wasn't even his physical response to her that nagged at him. Clara Sinclair's spirit was so different from the people who littered his royal life that it tugged at him. Made him hanker for a life he could never have.

Marcelo didn't have a clue how Clara had managed to squeeze herself into Alessia's dress.

'Can you even breathe in that?' he asked, trying very hard not to stare at her breasts so clearly delineated beneath the red fabric. Thankfully Alessia had taken his warning of Clara's lack of underwear seriously and had chosen a material and colour that didn't have the slightest hint of transparency to it.

She sucked her cheeks in and widened her eyes, then laughed. 'Just.'

'You can borrow something of mine if it would be more comfortable?'

'Fashion isn't supposed to comfortable,' she dismissed.

'You have nothing on your feet.'

'Then we'll just have to go to a shoe shop.'

'Can't you borrow a pair of Alessia's?'

His sister coughed.

'My feet are two sizes bigger than Princess Twinkletoes,' Clara explained.

'Don't worry,' Alessia said. 'I've already called ahead to Bonitas. We'll go through the private entrance. She won't have to walk on the streets barefoot.'

'How much spending money do I get?' Clara asked.

Marcelo strode to the glass table in the corner where his private secretary had left the items he'd ordered before he went to bed. 'I've set you up with an unlimited credit card.'

'What does that mean?'

'That you can spend whatever you like. There is no limit.'

Doubt rang in her voice. 'But there has to be a limit.'

'Not with this card.' He passed it to her.

She studied it with suspicion before a hint of mischief came into her eyes. 'You realise that if it's true and this really is unlimited then I'm going to take advantage of it?'

'That's the whole point. I want you to go shopping and buy everything that catches your eye. Anything you want. Don't look at the prices.'

The smile she bestowed him with made him feel like he'd grown three feet.

Clara watched one of the guards who'd accompanied her and Alessia on their shopping trip load all her new possessions in the boot of the car. Soon, the other car that had accompanied them—Alessia was a princess and so needed protection—was being loaded too.

It had been the most fantastic shopping trip of her entire life. Even better, she'd had company for it, something she'd not had since she was an adolescent and her brother had made his housekeeper take her shopping when she needed new clothes and stuff. To go shopping with a friend had been wonderful and she very much hoped it was something they would do again in her year in Ceres.

They were welcomed back at the castle by a horde of reporters at the gate to the Berruti family's private entrance. Pressing her face to the window in fascination, Clara was almost blinded by the flash of cameras.

'They're here for you,' Alessia said.

'What for?'

'What do you think?'

'Oh, yes, I'm the girl hanging from the helicopter in the arms of her prince. I suppose that makes me newsworthy.'

She'd have to get Marcelo to send that picture to her as soon as she got the new phone she'd bought set up. It had been like looking at a picture from a movie still, with the suave Knight in Black Tuxedo securely holding the ragged woman he'd just saved. Clara's only disappointment—apart from her bum looking big—was that the photographer had failed to capture Bob in it.

When the cars came to a stop, three men descended on them and efficiently emptied Clara's purchases so all she was left to carry was her new swanky handbag, which had cost more than her monthly salary.

After hugging Alessia and thanking her for being such great company, Clara opened the door into Marcelo's quarters.

She found him in his private garden with Bob, catching the last of the day's sun on his terrace. He barely moved a muscle from his seat at the outdoor table when she made her grand entrance.

'Ta-da,' she said and did a twirl. 'What do you think?'

Bob told her what he thought before Marcelo did, dashing over to paw at her ankles.

'That's a nice dress,' Marcelo finally answered.

'Isn't it?' she agreed, delighted with her dress but less than delighted with Marcelo's guarded expression. She'd hoped for a bit more enthusiasm for a dress that she'd completely disregarded his advice for and looked at the price of. Even she in all her excitement had baulked at spending two months' salary on a dress but only for a few seconds. She'd never felt such soft silken material against her skin before or checked her reflection out at every mirror and window she subsequently passed. 'Between you and me, I needed to get out of Alessia's dress. At one point I lost all feeling in my boobs. How's your day been?'

There was the faintest twitch of his lips. 'Busy.'

'Booked a date for our wedding?'

'All set for four weeks yesterday.'

'I'll pop it in my diary so I don't forget,' she teased, and was rewarded with the expressionless gorgeous face breaking into a shaking head smile. That was better. She liked it when Marcelo smiled. It set off a warm glow in her belly. 'Anything you need me to do?'

'No.' He looked at his watch. 'Dinner will be ready in thirty minutes.'

'Oh, good, I'm starving, and it means we've got time for you to check out what I've bought.'

'Didn't Alessia check it all for you?'

'Yep. She was great, but it's your arm I'll be seen on and I don't want to embarrass you by wearing things you find unsuitable.' Clara was determined to be the best public wife she could be to this daring and generous man. Even though he'd failed to go shopping with her, he'd spent so much time in her head that day he might as well have been there. Every item she'd bought had been with Marcelo's face in mind hoping he'd like it as much as she did. 'Also, I have a surprise for you.'

He raised a questioning eyebrow and got to his feet.

Itching to dive through all her purchases, Clara skipped up the stairs.

All her new stuff had been laid neatly in her dressing room. Her mum had had a dressing room too, much smaller than this but, to little Clara, it had been the most fascinating place on earth. An old memory flashed through her of sitting at the dressing table and smearing red lipstick on and trying to use it as blush like she'd seen her mum do and then prancing into the bedroom to show it off. Her mum, who'd been in bed with another of her many headaches, had told her she looked like a beautiful clown.

'What are you thinking?' Marcelo asked, noticing how Clara had seemed to have retreated into her own world. Usually, she was so *present*. He supposed that's why his quarters had felt so still without her. Only one day in her company and her absence had been tangible.

She blinked and met his stare with a smile. 'About my mum.'

'Am I right thinking she's not with us any more?' he asked carefully.

'She's dead if that's what you mean?'

'I'm sorry.'

'People always say that,' she mused. 'That they're sorry. Why is that, do you think?'

Disarmed at the question, he shrugged and answered as honestly as he could. 'To be polite?'

'As a form of social nicety?'

'When you put it like that, yes.'

'That's what I thought. I mean, you didn't know my mum, so why would you be sorry that she died?'

'Sorry for *you*.' And sorry that she could ask such a question. 'How old were you when it happened?'

'Six.'

He winced. Younger than he'd guessed. 'And your father?'

'He died of a massive stroke when I was twelve, but you don't need to be sorry about that for me. I haven't cried for him since his funeral.'

It was a comment that momentarily dumbfounded him, reminding him of how she'd so blithely informed him that she'd have to wait until she joined her father in hell before getting an apology from him.

How could this woman of all people imagine she'd be going to hell? And what had her father done to make her think he was already there and stop her shedding any tears for him once he'd been laid to rest?

Before he could put any of these thoughts into words, Clara, who'd been unpacking boxes, waved an arm at the items she'd laid out like a fan on the dressing room sofa, and chewed on her bottom lip. 'So, what do you think? Tell me if you think I got carried away. I didn't mean to buy so much but the clothes were all so fabulous and having no spending restraints went to my head—honestly, I earn a pittance at home…but in fairness, I do get free accommodation, but my actual wages are tiny so I don't have much to spare on clothes and normally buy second-hand in charity shops—'

'Clara,' he interrupted.

'Hmm?'

'You don't have to explain yourself. The credit card is unlimited for a reason and is yours to keep. Go mad with it whenever you want. I've arranged for you to have your own driver so whenever you want to go shopping or leave the castle for any reason, all you have to do is summon him and he will take you.'

Her eyes widened. 'Are you serious?'

'Yes. There's a team of palace protection officers ready to accompany you too. I don't want you to feel trapped in any way.'

'You are the kindest, most thoughtful man. And after you let me spend all that money...' She shook her head in wonderment.

'I'm not doing it to be kind,' he felt compelled to tell her. 'You have to remember, in less than a month you are going to be my wife and will have the title of princess. All eyes will be on you.' They would be on her whether she was a princess or not. He didn't imagine Clara could walk down a street without turning heads.

She bit into her lip again then, almost shyly, said, 'So what *do* you think? Are these clothes suitable for a princess?'

Recognising that his opinion really did matter to her, he smiled. 'Yes, *bella*. They are as beautiful as the princess who will be wearing them.'

All as beautiful as the dress currently wrapped around her curvy body, a vibrant red-and-yellow-checked sixties vibe creation that suited her personality as much as it suited her looks, with a high neck, short sleeves and a hem that came to mid-thigh. When she'd appeared in his garden he'd had to stop himself from doing a double take, not just from how ravishing she looked but from the glow of happiness that had suffused her. It was a glow he'd longed to touch, and he'd had to root himself to his seat and force his features to remain neutral to counter it.

Colour spread over her cheeks and, for the first time, she flittered her stare away from him, only for a moment, but as her stare was normally so implacably bold, it was noticeable.

'When we're in public will we have to pretend to be in love?' she asked, lifting the lid of another box.

'Do you think you can?'

She caught his eye and, her cheeks back to their normal colour, grinned. 'I will give it my best shot.'

'Explain something to me,' he said, asking one of the many questions about his soon-to-be wife that had occupied his thoughts that day. 'How can you be okay going along with such a public lie when you're clearly honest to your bones?'

She considered the question a moment before reaching for another box. 'We're marrying for real so that isn't a lie. The end of our marriage won't be a lie either—I *am* homesick. And I won't be telling any lies, will I? Your palace press machine will be doing all that. I'll only be acting when we're in public together, and while I don't think I'll be able to act as if I'm in love with you, I'll definitely be able to act like I fancy you, which should look like the same thing because in case you haven't noticed, I find you remarkably attractive, so that won't be a lie either.'

Dio, her nonchalance in the way she admitted her attraction! That was a turn-on in itself, and the heat simmering in his veins, which he'd been doing his utmost to ignore, ramped up four notches.

Clenching his jaw, Marcelo dragged his stare away from Clara's face only to find it locked on the open box in her hands. It contained a set of lacy red underwear.

Following the movement of his stare, she grinned and put the box down without removing the garments. 'An improvement on the bra I wore yesterday, eh?'

He cleared his constricted throat and did everything in his power to stop himself thinking of Clara wearing those skimpy items but his willpower was no match for his rabid imagination and, to his horror, heat pooled in his groin and tightened his loins.

'Quite,' he said, having to speak through a jaw he didn't dare unclench. 'Come on, leave that. I'll get the staff to put it away for you.'

'Not a chance—I've been looking forward to doing it myself, thank you very much.' Lifting the lid of yet another box, she shot her happy stare back at him. 'Here it is.'

'What?'

'Your surprise.' She handed the box to him. 'A present for you.'

Now he really was dumbfounded. 'You've bought *me* a gift?'

'It's not much,' she said, and to his astonishment she looked shamefaced. 'I'm afraid I don't know you well enough to know what gifts you'd like and Alessia was no help whatsoever. She was useless.'

'You didn't have to buy me anything.'

'I wanted to. You've done so much for me...'

Marcelo forced his jaw to relax but he could still hear the tension in his voice. 'How many times do I have to tell you that you're the one doing me the favour here and that your agreement to marry me far outweighs any debt you feel you owe me?'

'We're going to have to agree to disagree there but even if I did agree with you I would still have wanted to get you something. When my mum used to go shopping she always brought me a present back with her and it always made me feel...'

Clara shook her head. How hard it was to vocalise something as simple as a gift received. The warm glow that would spread from her chest knowing she'd been thought of. It was a feeling so long ago and distant that remembering it sent a pang through her. She hadn't mattered enough to anyone for surprise gifts since her mother died. But that was okay, she told herself. She didn't need gifts. She had everything she needed. Life was good.

'What she made me feel was a nice feeling and I wanted you to have that feeling too,' she continued. 'Are you going to open it? I have receipts in case you hate them.'

He lifted the lid. In it was two smaller boxes. One contained a belt, the other a pair of cufflinks in the shape of a ball and chain.

'The belt is to replace the one you trashed last night trying to make it fit me,' she explained, standing close to him. She caught a whiff of his lovely warm scent. He really did smell wonderful. Too wonderful. So wonderful he was making her salivate.

Confused at the strange feelings rushing through her, she edged away a little and said, 'The other is a bit of a joke, but a joke meant with kindness.' She pulled a face, suddenly uncertain that he would get it. As a rule, people didn't get her or her jokes.

But then Marcelo's gaze lifted and met hers, and her heart swelled.

'I get it,' Marcelo said, unbelievably touched as well as amused.

'I thought you could wear them on our wed-

ding day. I'll try not to be your ball and chain,'
she assured him. 'I won't get in the way of
your life.'

'Yes, you will,' he contradicted. 'Just as I'm
going to be your ball and chain and get in the
way of your life. It's going to be you and me for
the next year, *bella*.'

Her eyes softened. 'I can think of worse men
to be chained to.'

And he could think of worse women too...

For a long moment nothing was said between
them, not until a burst of anxiety suddenly
creased her face. 'Before I forget, I bought myself a music system for my room. Is that okay?'

'For the last time, you do not have to ask per-
mission or justify your spending to me in any
way, shape or form.' Straightening, he added,
'Spend whatever you like whenever you like.'

'Thank you. I'm glad you said that because
I also bought myself a Ferrari.' She'd barely
finished telling him that when she burst into
a cackle of laughter. 'That was a joke. I can't
drive.' She stood suddenly still and stared at
him with widening eyes before her shoulders
jiggled. 'Can you teach me?'

'To drive?'

'Yes.'

He had a vision of them tearing over Ceres'
mountain range in one of his sports cars, the top
down, Clara's long hair streaming behind her,

laughter on her face, her hand on his lap, the new perfume she was wearing that he'd been doing his best to block from filling his senses, adrenaline pumping through them both…

He severed the image with a firm, 'No.'

'Why not? Can't you drive either?'

'I've been driving since I was sixteen.'

'Then why won't you teach me?'

'Because you would drive me nuts.' In too many ways.

She was not in the least perturbed at this. 'What if I promise to keep my mouth shut?'

'Are you capable of doing that?'

'There's only one way to find out…'

'Yes, and that's not when you're behind a wheel,' he told her firmly.

She laughed and skipped away from him to return to her purchases. 'And I thought you were a man who thrived on adventure.'

CHAPTER SIX

'WHEN DO YOUR parents get back?' Clara asked as she shared breakfast with Marcelo two days later on the garden terrace under the rising sun. Having lived in a flat above the animal shelter for six years, it was lovely to have a garden. Enclosed for complete privacy and beautifully maintained by the castle gardeners, she thought it wonderful.

She'd joined Marcelo ten minutes earlier and other than a quick glance at her appearance, a swift, 'Good morning,' and a pat on the head for Bob, he'd sipped at his *caffè latte* and picked at his pastry in silence whilst reading the news on his phone.

Her question didn't drag his gaze from his phone. 'A week on Friday.'

They'd flown to Australia on an official visit the day after Clara's arrival on Ceres. Seeing as she hadn't yet met them, she assumed the timing wasn't anything personal. 'When do you think I'll get to meet them?'

'I imagine a dinner will be arranged on their return. I know they're keen to meet you.'

She reached for a second chocolate brioche. She wondered how big her bum would get if she ate two chocolate brioches for breakfast every day for the next year. Marcelo, she'd noticed in her short time here, limited himself to only one. Marcelo, she also noticed, had so far conducted their conversation without looking at her. She didn't think he could be properly reading his phone as he was definitely listening to her with both ears. 'You'll have to teach me table etiquette.'

'Didn't they teach you that at school?'

'I skipped those lessons.'

That made him look from his phone to her.

She grinned mischievously. Clara liked it when she had Marcelo's full attention. It meant she could look at his gorgeous face. 'Those lessons were boring. What kind of conversation will they expect from me?'

His sensuous lips stretched into a smile. It amazed her how often she found her gaze drifting to them. When he'd taken her to the British embassy the day before to sort her passport out, there had been a moment when she'd been so caught up watching his mouth move as he spoke to the official that had speedily taken it upon himself to deal with her case—having a prince of the island at her side had certainly helped on that score—that she'd completed zoned out.

'Just normal, everyday conversation,' he said. 'Don't worry about it. In private they're pretty informal.'

'Only *pretty* informal?'

'They're from a generation where being royal meant formality. My mother was raised knowing she would be queen and was trained from birth for her role. She is modern in her outlook but that modernity sometimes clashes with the values and sensibilities she was raised with.'

'I hope I don't say or do anything to offend her. She's going to be my mother-in-law for a year so I imagine it would be a bit awkward if she decides she hates me. I mean, what if she's wearing a really horrible dress and asks me if I like it? Would she do something like that? Some people do and then when you tell them the truth, they get all huffy. I don't get it. Why ask for an opinion if you don't want a truthful answer? Isn't that dishonest? To ask the question in the first place, I mean.'

Marcelo smothered an inward sigh and put his phone down. He'd had a terrible night's sleep. It had taken him longer than normal to get off and then he'd pulled himself awake from a dream involving Clara and the red lace underwear he'd caught a glimpse of in her dressing room. Every time he'd closed his eyes after that, the dream had remained vivid, the knowledge she lay in a bed only a wall away feeding it. Lord knew when he'd drifted back off but the end result was he felt decidedly unrefreshed and then, within minutes of sitting down for some sustenance, the woman who'd prevented his sleep had appeared on the garden terrace all sleepy-eyed and tousle-haired and dressed in a pair of perfectly modest silk pyjamas that showed perfectly well her lack of underwear. He couldn't see anything he shouldn't but the way the silk caressed her curves meant it didn't need to be transparent. It had taken approximately one second for his loins to react.

However, ignoring Clara, even to get a grip on his increasing hunger for her, was not an option. He had a year of this to look forward to. He had to get used to it.

But damn, it was hard not to look at her and react, not when she was so damn sexy. Look at her now, her chair pushed back from the table, one knee pulled up to her chest, unashamedly devouring her brioche. What man's blood wouldn't burn at such a sight?

Pushing his plate to one side, he said, 'Do you ever tell white lies?'

She ripped off a piece of her brioche. 'No. A lie's a lie.' The brioche disappeared between the plump lips that had also featured heavily in his dream.

'Not even to spare someone's feelings? To make them feel good about themselves or better in themselves?'

She swallowed her bite with a shrug. 'I don't like to hurt people's feelings. I try very hard and not always successfully to live by the maxim of *If you've nothing good to say then don't say anything at all*, but I can't tell a lie. The consequences can be very bad.'

'The voice of experience?' he queried idly, taken with the tiny crumb lodged in the corner of that amazingly kissable mouth.

She nodded. 'My mother died of a brain tumour. Did you know that?'

Taken aback at her words, he blinked sharply to pull his focus away from her mouth. 'No.'

'She was ill for a long time. Everyone knew. But no one told me.' Clara compressed the pointless churn in her belly. There was no point getting upset about something that happened so long ago.

She rarely spoke about her mother's death, not because she didn't want to but because people so rarely asked. Of course, Marcelo hadn't asked but she figured this was a story he needed to know. She wanted him to know.

'She would spend days in bed with terrible headaches and I thought it was normal, and I thought it was normal for mummies to sometimes go to hospital for long spells for their headaches. I thought it was normal because that's what I was told. But I knew what death was because I remember visiting her once with my father and asking him if she was going to die and he said *no*. I distinctly remember him telling me that she'd be better soon, and I believed him. When she was home, I would get into bed with her every morning and cuddle her and, if her head wasn't hurting too much, we would watch cartoons together, and I had no idea that she would soon be taken from me because I believed my father's lies and all the other people who lied too. Right until the end they kept the lie going, even when she weighed little more than I did and was too weak to raise her head. I lived in a house with death hovering over us and I was the only one who couldn't see it because I believed their lies. I was the only one who didn't get the chance to say goodbye to her.'

To that day, Clara couldn't say why she'd never asked her mother but was glad she hadn't. She didn't think she'd be able to endure knowing her mother had lied too.

Marcelo's heart thumped painfully but so coldly into the ice that had filled the cavity of his chest.

All too clearly he could envisage Clara as a six-year-old child trying her best to be quiet and not make her mummy's head hurt any more than it already did. He could envisage it clearly because he remembered his sister at that age. Alessia was seven years younger than him and when she'd been six, Marcelo thirteen and Amadeo fifteen, their parents had gone on a state visit to New Zealand over the Easter period for a month while the boys had been home from school. Alessia had missed their mother so much she'd spent days inconsolable. Marcelo had seen it as his job to cheer his baby sister up. It was that time, he was sure, that had forged the closeness between the two of them.

He closed his eyes and tried to get air into his closed lungs. 'Do you think they lied because they were trying to protect you? You were very young.'

'I'm sure that's how they justified it to themselves,' she answered matter-of-factly. 'My brother said as much when I asked him about it once.'

That would be the same brother who'd sold her to a man rumoured to hit women. The same brother whose name Marcelo had searched two nights before when he couldn't sleep. What he'd discovered had enraged him. Andrew Sinclair was worth fifty million pounds. He'd been the sole heir of their father's will. A few calls later and he'd learned that Terence Sinclair had made no financial provisions for his only daughter once she reached the age of eighteen. He'd left her fate entirely in the hands of the half-brother who hated her.

No wonder Clara believed her father had gone to hell.

Marcelo forced his focus to remain on the words Clara was saying rather than his rage at the men whose duty had been to care and protect her.

'But that doesn't change the outcome, does it?' she said. 'I went to her bedroom one morning for our cuddle, and her bed was empty. She'd died in the night. The undertakers collected her body while I was dreaming in my bed and I never saw her again.'

'Clara…' He shook his head, trying to clear it of the noise filling it. His breakfast churned violently in his stomach.

What she'd lived through would churn anyone's stomach.

She reached across the table and squeezed his fisted hand. Smiling kindly, she said, 'It's okay. You don't have to think of a platitude for me. I can see by your face that my story has upset you and I'm sorry for that. I didn't mean to ruin your breakfast.'

He loosened his hand and twisted it so he could squeeze her hand back. Gazing into her dark brown eyes that contained not a jot of self-pity, his guts cramped tightly.

Clearing his throat, he said, 'I am glad you told me.'

Her nose wrinkled. 'You don't look like you're glad about it.'

Any other time, he would have laughed at her astuteness and willingness to speak what she saw.

'Glad is the wrong word,' he conceded. 'But you are going to be my wife and a member of the Berruti royal family, and it is my job to protect you for the time you and I are together. Understanding you will make it easier for me to do that.'

She stared at him with ringing eyes and a faintly disbelieving expression for the longest time. 'You want to *protect* me?'

He squeezed her hand again without thinking.

Yes, he realised, a growing part of him did want to protect her. He'd thought Clara the woman least in need of protection and he still did think that, but his sister had been right— there was something about Clara that made you *want* to protect her. He couldn't put his finger on what that vulnerability was but it was there.

'You are giving up a year of your life for my family's sake,' he said. 'Protecting you is the least I can do. Understanding you will help me do that.'

'I *can't* lie,' she said simply. 'Even the thought of telling a lie makes me want to be sick.' A hint of mischief flashed in her eyes. 'I can't begin to tell you the amount of trouble telling the truth has got me into over the years.'

'I can imagine,' he said drily. 'How on earth have you held a job down for so long?'

'Because I spend most of my time with the animals, I'm great at my job and they pay me such a pittance it'd be hard to get anyone else, which is why I asked you to make that donation to them as they really need the boost in funds.' Then the mischief faded and her voice slowed and quietened. 'It's not just that I can't tell a lie. I can't bear to hear them either.'

'Understandable.'

Her fingers tightened around his. An urgency came into her voice. 'Promise you will never lie to me.'

Marcelo's guts cramped again. He didn't like to think of himself as a liar but, like most people, he told white lies to spare others' feelings and, sometimes, to spare his own. This might be the hardest promise to keep he'd ever made because Clara would view a white lie as seriously as any other lie. Taking a deep breath, he jerked a nod. 'I promise.'

Her shoulders and mouth loosened. 'Thank you. Trust is very hard for me but I want to go into our marriage giving you the benefit of the doubt, otherwise I think it would make life difficult for both of us. And, while we're discussing my many faults, if you hadn't already noticed, stress and heightened emotions tend to make my mouth run away with me even more than normal. I try to control it but I'm not always successful, so if we're on an official engagement and you notice me blabbing away like a roadrunner on speed, you might need to step in and shut me up.'

'Our first public engagement is planned for the weekend,' he informed her.

Alarm flashed. 'That soon?'

'The world needs to see us together. We're going to have a pre-wedding party the week before the wedding which will be a much more formal affair, so this will be a good primer for you. It's a closed, select event at the Agon embassy so a good way for you to get a taste of a royal engagement without overwhelming you.'

'But I'm not ready, even for a primer. I don't care if I embarrass myself but I don't want to embarrass you.'

'We have four days to make a start. Your tutors—experts in decorum and etiquette—start tomorrow so that will get the basics covered. We can come up with tactics to curb your roadrunner mouth and then we'll stay out of sight until the pre-wedding party and work in more detail with you.'

Her eyes gleamed and she giggled. 'That sounds like a lot of work. Sure you still want to marry me?'

Glad of the lightening of the mood, he went along with it. 'It's too late now—the press release announcing it went out yesterday. I think, though, we might have to take some preventative measures to make sure you're never on the receiving end of reporters' personal questions.'

'Very wise,' she agreed approvingly. 'And probably wise to warn your mum not to ask me if her bum looks big.'

Welcome laughter welled in him. Marcelo tugged her hand to his mouth and kissed the knuckles lightly. 'I will warn her.' And his father and siblings. He didn't think Alessia could know the details of Clara's mother's death.

'Thank you. Can I have my hand back now please? It feels very nice you holding it but I need to take a shower. Are you okay to watch Bob for me?'

Resisting the temptation to kiss her hand again, he released it. It disturbed him how much he wanted to keep hold of it. 'Sure.'

He was helpless to stop himself from watching her pad back inside. Helpless to stop his eyes fixing on the delectable bottom so vividly delineated beneath the silk.

When she stepped over the threshold, she paused and looked back at him.

Her shoulders rose sharply then dropped. A smile formed. And then she turned again and disappeared.

Marcelo cradled his head then covered his face and tried hard not to imagine Clara naked in the shower.

How was it possible for one woman, in the space of one conversation, to evoke so many feelings in him? Feelings that cut to the bone. Feelings that made him want to jump out of an aeroplane with her strapped to his back sharing the rush of adrenaline and then hold her tight and shield her from the dangers of the world, slay a dragon to protect her and then lay her on a bed and devour her.

The next year was going to be long.

It was going to be torture.

Clara was apprehensive about meeting the priest who'd be marrying them but, after three days of intense princess training, her brain was frazzled. There was so much to learn, from the little things like posture and not fidgeting to the bigger things like how to address dignitaries. On paper, she supposed it all looked slightly pointless and unnecessary, because seriously, who cared about decorum and etiquette in this day and age? But that was the point—it mattered to Marcelo and his family, and so it mattered to her. She was only a day away from being introduced to the world as an imminent member of the Berruti royal family and the last thing she wanted was to embarrass Marcelo by getting things wrong. She'd already had one vivid dream where she entered an embassy dressed to the nines but with her dress tucked into her knickers, so to give her brain a break from it all was welcome.

The chapel was tucked away behind the castle. To reach it, they passed the ancient amphitheatre, Marcelo pointing out numerous grottos and reflecting pools and, far in the distance, the ancient maze that still delighted visitors of all ages.

Up close, the chapel loomed taller than she'd expected, and she entered it with a thudding heart.

In three weeks and one day, she and Marcelo would make their marriage vows in here.

It was a thought that made her shiver but, oddly, not unpleasantly. So many odd feelings had enveloped her since her arrival here. They were all linked to Marcelo.

Somehow, in the course of a week, Clara had become attuned to another human's presence. Become used to sharing her meals with a hunky two-legged creature rather than furry four-legged ones. Used to Marcelo's watchful presence in her princess lessons. Used to his supressed smiles when she said something her decorum teacher considered—that dreaded word—*inappropriate*. She'd even got used to him having had enough of her company by nightfall and retiring to bed as soon as their evening meal was finished.

She quite understood why he needed space from her. Clara had known since she was a little girl that she could be too much for most people.

She knew he didn't go straight to sleep as when she took herself to bed hours later each evening she'd see a glow of light under his door. Once, with her heart beating fast, she'd put her ear to his door and heard his television. And that was the one thing she was struggling to understand—why her heart beat so erratically around him. Before Marcelo had come into her life she'd never given her heart a second thought; it was just another organ in her body quietly getting on with its job of keeping her alive.

It was beating erratically now as she gazed up at the high, domed roof and the vast yet intricate stained-glass windows with Marcelo standing so close. Loud, echoing thuds against her ribs.

Wrapping her arms around her chest, she took a seat on a pew and broke the silence. 'I thought chapels were supposed to be small?'

'My ancestor who had it built was intensely religious,' he replied, sitting beside her. 'He would have been a monk if he hadn't been heir to the throne.'

'What would you have done if you hadn't

been born a prince? Would you still have joined the army?'

He rubbed the back of his neck. 'I don't know. I joined because I itched for adventure before taking up royal duties full-time and the military is considered a worthy job for a royal to take. Royal life is incredibly dull—be thankful you only have to put up with it for a year. Amadeo always wanted to be a racing driver but that was out of the question.'

'Too dangerous?'

'Yes.'

Was her awareness of Marcelo's muscular thigh only inches from hers dangerous? Was the temptation to place her hand on it dangerous?

Clara had never felt temptation of a sensual kind before she'd met Marcelo.

The look she often caught in his eyes before he blinked it away, like he wanted to devour her, felt dangerous too. Thrillingly, excitingly dangerous.

What would it feel like to be kissed by him? Would it be nice? Or would it repulse her? Or, worst of all, would she feel nothing?

If they did ever kiss, would he find it nice or repulsive or boring?

Probably it was best to never find out. As things stood, they had a great relationship—the best relationship she'd had with a human since Alessia. Why ruin it over something as tedious as desire? That's if what she even felt for him was desire. Maybe it was just curiosity brought about by being thrown together and their proximity. That he was so ruddy handsome and sexy only added to the mix.

'Did you enjoy your time in the army?' she asked, the first question to come into her head for distraction against the awareness licking her skin, an awareness that really was inappropriate in a house of God.

'I loved it. There's great camaraderie and adventure in the military. I'd hoped to stay until I was forty.'

'What happened?'

'Nothing dramatic. I got a chest infection that developed into pneumonia. Laid me up for months and weakened my body enough that I was no longer able to do my job effectively, so I was medically discharged.'

'That sounds dramatic to me.' Dramatic enough for her heart to make a strange icy swoop...

At the audible shock in Clara's voice, Marcelo faced her. 'I recovered so not dramatic,' he assured her, 'but it took a lot of work to rebuild my strength. I'm fighting fit now, but it took over a year before I was back to full health.'

How he'd hated those long months, rebuilding his strength for a life of duty and tedium, the career he'd loved gone, the life he'd loved over.

'Was your life in danger?'

'At one point, yes.'

'Then that's definitely dramatic. Why didn't the media report it? I mean, you're a prince so that would have been newsworthy, wouldn't it?'

'The life of a royal is a life of scrutiny.' That was another thing he'd loved about the military—the anonymity, that he could be himself without having to worry about anything he said or did being reported or scrutinised.

His discharge didn't just terminate his career but his freedom to be him, Marcelo the man rather than Marcelo the prince.

Sitting here, properly alone with Clara for the first time in days, close enough to feel the heat of her body and smell her sultry perfume, he was very much aware of his mortal side. The primitive side. Responding to her perfume and the heat of her skin...

Clenching his fists on his lap, he took a deep breath before continuing. 'The press can be rabid and as far as I was concerned my illness and recovery was a private matter. My family and colleagues knew my wish for discretion so...' A thought suddenly occurred to him and he twisted his face to her. 'How do you know the press didn't report it?'

'Because I would have read it. I've read all the reports that caught my eye about you since I was fifteen.' Her eyes gleamed with amusement as she explained. 'I saw you pick Alessia up from school once. I thought it was a really nice thing, you taking her out—my brother didn't visit me once when I was at school. She told me after that you often took her out when you were on leave. I've kept an eye out for your name ever since because I wanted to assure myself your life was going well. I like it when good things happen to good people. But don't worry, I wasn't cyber stalking you in particular. I did the same for Alessia too.'

'So that's how you recognised me?' he murmured, but whatever she said in answer was lost through the sudden rush of blood pounding in his head as he gazed into the dark brown eyes that did something to him.

Clara did something to him.

The tempo of his heart became a burr, thickening his blood to a heavy sludge.

Her eyes pulsed. Colour rose on her cheeks. Their faces were so close he could hear the raggedness of her breath.

She was so damned irresistible...

You're in a house of God.

Swallowing hard, he turned his gaze to the door that led into the priest's private domain. As if summoned by Marcelo's will, the door opened.

Marcelo finally released the breath he'd been holding.

It took a long time before he felt controlled enough to meet Clara's stare again.

Before she could answer, the priest emerged.

CHAPTER SEVEN

THERE WERE NO princess lessons the next day. Instead, Clara had to endure two hours of tedium with a world-famous designer who clearly thought she was God's gift to wedding dresses. An hour of that time was spent acting like a human mannequin while her measurements were taken.

It had been exactly a week since Marcelo had rescued her from her fate and whisked her to Ceres and this was the first time she'd been bored.

No, she admitted. Not bored. Restless.

She couldn't stop thinking about the moment she'd held her breath in anticipation of Marcelo kissing her. But it had been only a fleeting blink of a moment, passing so quickly she wasn't even sure whether or not she'd imagined it.

Wishful thinking?

She shivered.

'Can you keep still?' the designer scolded.

'Sorry.'

Focus, she told herself. Consider standing like a mannequin good practice for that evening's function when she'd have to put her new princess face on.

But no matter how hard she tried, she couldn't stop her mind lurching back to Marcelo. She wondered how he was getting on in Milan, where he'd flown to after breakfast to arrange his own wedding outfit.

When the measurements were done and the designer reached, again, for her bulging portfolio, inspiration to get rid of her struck.

'How many wedding dresses have you made, in total?' she asked.

'I have lost count. About one hundred and three.'

Clara wasn't quick enough to hide her cackle of laughter. 'Then you must have a good idea what suits individual women?'

'Of course.'

'Then why don't you let your imagination go wild on this dress for me? I definitely want the skirt of the dress to be like a meringue and I don't want the top part to be heart-shaped…' Not when she'd had a heart-shaped wedding dress for King Pig. 'And I'd like to look like a proper princess for the day—a bit like Cinderella when she goes to the ball—but those are my only stipulations. You're the expert. You must know what will and won't suit me. Use all your knowledge and experience and create something you think is fit for a princess for me.'

After a bit more cajoling and flattering, the designer finally agreed. By the time she left, she actually seemed excited to be given a free rein. Clara suspected most of the women she created wedding dresses for turned into Bridezilla.

Finally alone, Clara took Bob into the garden for some training, clutching her phone in case Marcelo called or messaged. He'd said he'd be back by lunch. It was almost three p.m.

Being here felt very strange without him. Very strange. And it was strange too how keenly she felt his absence, how her ears had pricked up at every external noise as if it could be him returning, how her stare kept gluing itself to the door waiting for him to throw it open.

There was no sign of him when she went back inside an hour later. Swallowing the icy feeling forming in her heart she went through her phone and selected the playlist she'd spent hours creating, pressed the button indicating the living room and then pressed shuffle. Seconds later, music piped out of the four corners of the room where the staff had rigged up speakers for her.

Where was he?

She'd give it another ten minutes and then call him. With the number of bodyguards who accompanied his every step out of the palace she was sure he was fine, but the icy feeling was spreading.

A song came on that she adored and she sang along, trying even harder to tamp down the icy worry in her chest. The palace beauty team would be here soon to turn her into a princess for the night but there was no sign of her prince.

Where was he?

She sang even louder.

'Having fun?'

Startled, she spun around and found Marcelo standing at the threshold of the living room wearing one of those snug T-shirts she liked so much matched with a pair of black jeans. His almost black hair was as perfectly coiffured and groomed as it had been when he'd left the castle and just to look at him made her heart bloom with pleasure as well as relief and delight. 'You're back!'

The smile on Clara's face was like no smile Marcelo had been on the receiving end of before. Not from his family. Not from any of his lovers.

No one had ever looked at him like that.

The smile still alight on her face, she added, 'I didn't hear you come in.'

He worked hard to keep his tone neutral over the thumping of his heart. 'Hardly surprising with all this noise.'

Marcelo had flown to Milan needing breathing space from Clara. Breathing space from the battle raging inside himself. Hours spent every day with a woman who made his blood burn, trapped in her zany orbit, hearing her frequent laughter, watching her face screw in concentration as she undertook what she called her princess lessons, retiring to bed early every night because the buzz in his veins deepened when night fell and they were left alone together, finding no solace in his bedroom, too alert for the tread of her steps and the creak of her bedroom door, eyes glued to the wall separating them...

His awareness of her was rapidly consuming him but it wasn't his growing hunger that had seen him escape his island for some respite. It was Clara's spirit, that unquantifiable something that sparkled from her and sang to the part of him prone to rushes of blood to his head and impulsive behaviour.

The part of him that had no place in his life any more.

Clara and this whole situation was his responsibility. Marcelo's impulsive actions had put the monarchy in its greatest peril in two centuries. He needed to keep his head and, to do that, he needed to keep Clara at arm's length. He needed to fight.

The problem was what he needed to do and what it was possible to do were two different things. How did you keep someone so full of life and joy, someone so *present*, at arm's length? Especially when you wanted them so much it hurt.

And especially when they smiled at you the way Clara smiled at him, with her whole, beautiful face.

'Sorry.' She turned the volume down with her phone. 'Better?'

'Yes. I can now hear myself think,' he said wryly, then shook his head. 'I would never have had you down as someone who likes sentimental love songs.'

'Love songs are the *best*,' she enthused.

How long would it take before she ceased to amaze him? Clara had to be the least sentimental person he'd met in his life and he'd found her singing and swaying to a song about unrequited love. She'd been oblivious to his presence and so he'd had a few moments of private observation watching the movements of her body, her curves softly showing through her white fitted calf-length trousers and multi-coloured long-sleeved top, dark blond hair loose and spilling over her shoulders. In those unobserved moments there had been an inexplicable tightening in his chest that had been far more acute than the tightening in his loins.

His loins were far easier to control.

And then she'd spun around and the look on her face when she'd seen him...

'How did you get on with the designer?' he asked.

'Great! I managed to get rid of her by giving her free rein on it.'

He laughed. 'I thought you'd love being involved in the creation process.'

She pulled a face. 'Turns out I much prefer choosing from finished products. Did you get your outfit sorted?'

'I did. And while I was there...' Filling his lungs with air, Marcelo stepped over to her. 'I bought something for you.'

Her eyes lit up, which was something considering there was a permanent light in them. 'A present?'

'An engagement ring.'

Marcelo had left his favourite tailor with the details for his wedding suit efficiently sorted, enjoying his breathing space away from Clara. And then he'd noticed the adjoining jewellery shop. He already knew Clara's ring size from when it had been measured for her wedding ring. Choosing an engagement ring would take five minutes of his time. Well, it would have if his impulsive decision hadn't turned into an obsessive quest to find *the* perfect ring for her. He'd visited six exclusive jewellers before the perfect ring revealed itself.

She was practically bouncing on her toes. 'Can I see?'

Doubt over whether she'd like it kicked in. His heart thumped hard as he opened the lid for her.

After what felt like a whole era had passed, she tore her gaze from the ring to him.

'That's for me?' Clara whispered, struggling to work her vocal chords.

Throat moving, he nodded. 'If you don't like it, tell me. I can return it. We can go shopping together and choose one you like.'

'But I do like it.'

'You do?'

Her heart was fit to burst. 'It's the most beautiful thing I've ever seen. Is it really for me?'

'Do you see another woman here in need of an engagement ring?'

His attempt at a joke brought a smile to her face. And set an unbidden tear trickling down her cheek.

'I thought you liked it?' he said, brow crinkling with confusion.

She wiped the tear away and sniffed and laughed at the same time. 'I *do*. I love it. I just can't believe you've chosen something so beautiful for little old me.' No one had ever gifted her anything so beautiful before. She hadn't received a present in years, not a proper meaningful gift that wasn't part of her work's Secret Santa.

Not knowing why her eyes were leaking, she wiped another tear away.

'Are you going to try it on?' he asked.

She held her hand out to him. 'I want you to put it on me.'

She felt rather than saw his hesitation. 'Please?' she said. 'I'm never going to have this moment again.'

Clara would never marry for real. She wasn't capable of forming the kind of bond that marriage followed—how could she when all trust had been knocked out of her at such a young age? For real bonds to form, trust was needed. Trust that they would never lie to you and trust that they had your best interests in their heart, and only her mum had ever had her best interests at heart. In any case, she doubted there was a man alive who could put up with her! But here, in this moment, she wanted to experience the romance of a ring being slid on her finger. Just for the experience. Just for the moment. And just with Marcelo...

It was comments like that which had fed Marcelo's determination for the perfect ring. Her honesty. Her lack of guile. Her lack of self-pity. Her matter-of-factness that relationships, never mind marriage, were not for her.

How easy it would have been for her to become bitter at what life had thrown at her but Clara latched on to the good rather than focus on the bad. Look how she'd spent her time in Ceres focusing on training to be a princess rather than indulging in bitterness and recriminations at the heinous behaviour of her brother and the King of Monte Cleure.

Surely it must affect her? Her brother had sold her to a monster who would have forced her into a marriage from which she would have been lucky to escape with her life, but, other than the time she'd opened up about how she'd been prepared to fight to her last breath on her wedding night, you'd never know what she'd been through.

There had been myriad reasons for him to buy her the perfect ring but deeper than all of them had been the need to do something special for her.

He'd had a strong feeling that it had been a long time since anyone had done anything special for her.

He attempted another joke. 'Do you want me to get down on one knee too?'

She pulled a humorous face. 'Let's not go overboard.'

Chuckling, he carefully plucked the fifteen-carat oval diamond set on an elegant pavé band covered in sparkling diamonds from the box and took hold of her hand.

The thumping of his heart became a boom.

He put the ring to her slender wedding finger. He'd never noticed what pretty hands Clara had before. Was it his imagination or was there a tremor in it?

Slowly, he slid the ring over her knuckle until it nestled snugly on her finger. The diamond glittered.

He lifted his gaze from the ring to her eyes. They shone as brightly as the jewel on her hand but the expression in them was one he hadn't seen before.

'It's perfect,' she said. 'How did you guess I would like it?'

He rubbed his thumb over the main diamond. 'I was going to get something colourful and elaborate but when I saw this...' He took a deep breath. 'It's simple and solitary and sparkling and beautiful. Just like you.' And worth every cent of the money he'd splurged on it, which had cost more than he'd paid for his Bugatti. It was the single most expensive item he'd ever bought.

Clara's lungs practically closed from the rapid expansion of her heart.

'Are you calling me simple?' she tried to jest, but it came out too choked to be funny. In its box, the ring had been stunning. On her finger, its beauty overwhelmed. It was an engagement ring fit for a real princess.

But, just like she would never be a real wife, she knew she could never be a real princess. Gazing at the sparkling diamond on her finger only reinforced that feeling. She would try, though. Try her darnedest to be the best princess she could be and make Marcelo proud and make herself at least a little worthy of this ring.

He squeezed his fingers around hers and gave something that was almost a smile. 'I meant it as a compliment. You have no artifice.'

'And that's a good thing?'

'At least I won't have to spend our marriage wondering what you're thinking.'

The overwhelming feelings finally became too much to contain and, tugging her fingers from his hold, she flung her arms around his neck. 'Thank you. I promise to take good care of it.'

She felt him stiffen but the erupting emotions were too strong for her to let go. Her nose had landed right below his collarbone and as she breathed in her senses were filled with the scent of Marcelo. It was a glorious scent, potent, masculine, a scent that burrowed inside her...

She barely registered the loosening of his body until his strong arms wrapped around her waist and pulled her tighter to him.

In the beat of a second it wasn't just his scent seeping through her senses.

In that beat of a second every nerve ending in her body shot to attention and Clara found that she was the one now stiffening as the beats of her heart quickened and sent hot blood surging through her veins.

The music changed. Another of the love songs she adored.

She needed to let go of him.

She wanted to move even closer.

The tips of her breasts were pressed against the hardness of his chest. There was a sensitivity in them she'd never known before.

Everything felt so heightened, like her senses had taken a double shot of caffeine. She pressed her cheek tighter into the top of his chest, filled her lungs with more of his scent and listened to the heavy thuds of his heart. She tried to swallow back the moisture filling her mouth but her throat didn't seem to be working properly. Nothing seemed to be working as it should. Her body had gone off-piste.

A hand swept deliciously up her back and threaded through her hair to cradle her head.

Slowly, Clara lifted her chin to look at him.

What she found on Marcelo's face slammed her heart against her ribs.

His jaw was set tight, his lips a tight, rigid line. His eyes…they were a darker blue than she had ever seen them and bore into hers with a hooded intensity that burned right into her core.

Suddenly, she couldn't breathe, too intent on the mouth closing in on hers to draw breath.

She could feel his breath whispering against her skin.

He was going to kiss her…

Her eyes fluttered shut as warm, firm lips brushed like a feather against hers.

Something deep inside her melted.

A loud knock on the living room door cut through the spell with the effect of a bucket of ice being tipped over her.

One moment she was locked in Marcelo's arms, the next she was five paces apart with no recollection of actually moving her feet or jellified legs.

'My apologies for the terrible timing,' Alessia said from the living room door, clearly embarrassed at having walked in on them at such an intimate moment. 'I've come to get Bob.'

For a moment Clara wondered what she was talking about and then it came to her. Alessia was dog-sitting for the night.

Events unfolded before Marcelo like he was watching from behind a screen. Clara, more flustered than usual, dashing around in search of all the puppy's stuff. Alessia's promise to bring the puppy back in the morning. Clara seeing them out.

And then she returned to the living room and the screen cleared.

Closing the door, she rested her back against it.

Their eyes clashed and held.

The silence was so complete you could hear a feather fall.

Colour rose high on her cheeks. Her chest rose slowly too then fell jaggedly. Her teeth sank into the plump bottom lip that had felt so incredible brushed against his.

He cleared his throat. 'Are you okay?'

She gave an overt blink. Her shoulders rose, her chin jutted and something that could have been a laugh flew from her mouth. 'I can't work out if I'm relieved or disappointed that Alessia interrupted us.'

This was such a classic piece of Clara honesty and so similar to what he was feeling that laughter swelled. 'Same.' What else could he do? Say it was a mistake?

Mistakes, no matter how fleeting, did not taste that good.

'Really?' A wide smile lit her face. Resting her head back against the door, she said, 'I'm glad it's not just me. I mean, I knew I found you attractive but any woman with eyes would find you attractive so I didn't think that was strange in itself, even though you're the only man I've ever found attractive, but now I have all these feelings running through me and...' She rubbed her arms. 'I don't know what to do. I mean, I've never kissed a man before.'

Something warm and thick that had nothing to do with desire filled his chest. 'Why not?'

'I've never wanted to. I've never been interested in men or sex. Don't get me wrong, I don't dislike men as a species or anything. It's just that I'm happy in my own company with my dogs and, to be honest, I've always found the thought of sex itself rather boring—I fast-forward sex scenes on TV.' Her teeth sank again into her bottom lip and her voice dropped. 'But now I think I must have changed in some way because there is something about you my body reacts to, and it keeps getting stronger. It's scary but…exciting, I think. So what about you? How do you feel? Because I'm not imagining that my feelings aren't one-sided, am I?'

There was such vulnerability in the way she posed this final question that he could only answer with the truth. 'No, *bella*, you're not imagining it.'

There came a point when a man had to admit defeat.

He must have been mad to think he could keep Clara at arm's length when in the space of a week she'd infected every waking moment. Even his nights weren't safe from her. She'd slipped into his dreams as if she'd always been there, and now that he'd experienced the thrill of her soft, sexy curves pressed against him and felt the tremble of her desire, his personal Rubicon had been crossed.

There was no going back. Not for him.

His hunger for Clara was too great to be contained any longer.

He wanted her. Every inch of her. In his arms and in his bed.

She blew out a puff of air and laughed tremulously. 'Oh, good. It'd be really embarrassing if you found me as attractive as a warthog after I've just unloaded all that on you.' She swallowed but didn't drop her stare. 'So what do we do about it?'

His every sinew tightened.

How easy it would be to close the space between them and show her what they should do about it, but instinct told him that would be a huge mistake.

There was a reason she was still standing across the room from him.

Clearing his throat, he said, 'That's up to you.'

Those mesmerising eyes stayed fixed on him for the longest time before her face broke out in another wide smile. 'In that case, I'm going to take a shower before the beauty team arrives.'

It took a beat for him to remember that they had their first official joint royal engagement that evening.

This was what Clara did to him. Made him forget himself.

'That will give me the time I need to think about whether we should take this any further.' She shook her head and stepped away from the door, rolling her eyes self-deprecatingly. 'Sorry, I know I do want to take it further. I just need to figure out if it's something we *should* do. And you should think about it too.'

And with that, she left the living room leaving Marcelo to his wild, tortured thoughts of the perilous turn his life could be about to take.

CHAPTER EIGHT

CLARA ADJUSTED THE band of her dress one last time before deciding she was ready. She hoped the ambassador's reception would be more exciting than it sounded. She hoped her boobs didn't fall out of her dress. She hoped her princess lessons paid off and she didn't embarrass Marcelo. Somehow, she had to contain the excitement that had been careering through her since their kiss that hadn't been quite a full-blown kiss but still a kiss. Excitement always made her motormouth worse and dulled her impulse control, and she had never, in her entire life, felt anything like this before.

She'd relived the moment approximately once every minute. Sometimes twice.

If Alessia hadn't interrupted them, how far would they have gone? How far would she have let it go?

The more pertinent question was how far did she *want* it to go? She knew her attraction for Marcelo had exploded. She knew she adored his company. She knew she adored him, and not just because he'd saved her life or brought her the most beautiful piece of jewellery in the world.

The problem was her complete lack of experience with men. Just because she'd liked being held in his arms and had practically swooned with desire at their way too brief kiss did not mean she'd like anything else. Just because the mere thought of his hands roaming her body sent thrills racing through her did not mean the reality would be anything like it.

And what about *his* expectations? Clara would never second-guess another person's thoughts.

Luckily she'd put all her jumbled questions in order by writing them down, and she shoved the note into her clutch bag before taking one last deep breath and leaving her bedroom.

She laughed when Marcelo took one look at her in the living room where he was waiting for her and his eyes practically fell out of his head.

'Now *that* is a reaction I like!' she said, delighted at such a visceral reaction.

He rose from the sofa. '*Dio*, *bella*, you look amazing. That dress…' He smacked a kiss to his fingers.

Loving the compliment, she beamed. 'You look amazing too. I keep thinking you should only wear jeans and T-shirts because you look so sexy in them but you're just as sexy in a tuxedo.'

His laugh sounded very much like a groan.

'Clara, I've spent the last two hours trying my best not to think sexy thoughts of you and then you come out with that while wearing a dress like that? Are you trying to kill me?'

'Let's wait until we've been married a few months before I try that, eh?'

Marcelo rubbed the back of his neck and suppressed another groan. He didn't see how he would make it to their wedding day without losing his mind, never mind a few months into it. Especially when Clara wore dresses like this one, a red velvet toga-style dress with the thick straps constituting the top half skimming either side of her full breasts to the diamond-studded sash tied around her waist. Her hair had been left loose, one side tucked behind her ear showing off diamond waterfall earrings. Her only other jewellery was her engagement ring. It sparkled as brightly as she did.

He could hear voices beyond the walls of the living room. His team were gathering.

'Ready to meet your public?' he asked.

'As ready as I'll ever be. Do you have a gag ready if needed?'

Stepping before her, Marcelo gazed deeply into the, oh, so expressive dark brown eyes. *Dio*, he longed to kiss her. Instead, he satisfied himself with tracing the back of a finger lightly down her cheekbone, and was gratified when her lashes fluttered and she shivered.

'You've got this, *bella*,' he assured her quietly, praying that he was right. 'The press will be camped outside the embassy and will take pictures of us together, but that will be your only contact with them. For the function itself, if you feel at any point that things are getting too much and that you're losing control, take my hand and squeeze it hard.'

'That sounds like a plan but you might find I spend the whole function squeezing it.'

'You've got this,' he repeated.

Her eyes softened. 'I hope so. For your sake.' And then a flare of the mischief he was becoming so familiar with flashed. 'Sure you don't want to bring a gag as backup? Just in case?'

Bursting into laughter, he took her hand and kissed the knuckles.

A short while later, they climbed into the back of their car. As Clara arranged herself next to him to minimise creases to her dress, Marcelo reflected that, for once, he was attending a royal function without dread of the certain tedium.

Whatever happened when they got home, whether she took the plunge and joined him in his bed or not, having Clara on his arm guaranteed the event would not be boring.

For that alone, he was grateful to have Clara Chaos in his life.

The reception was far more gruelling than Clara had anticipated. Held in the ambassador's residence in what looked from the outside to be a magnificent town house, it was filled with glamorous women and dashing men.

Trying to remember everything that had been drilled into her, especially the need to think before speaking, was a nightmare and much harder in practice than in theory.

They all wanted to talk to her. Funnily enough, everyone seemed to want to know about her relationship to the British royal family. There were more than a few crestfallen faces when she told them she'd never met anyone more senior than a viscount, and that had been at a garden party when she was a child.

'Why has no one asked me about King Pig?' she whispered to Marcelo when they had a brief respite from the deluge of interested people.

'They've been warned not to,' he murmured.

'Why?'

'Officially, because you're too traumatised to discuss it.'

'And unofficially?'

'Because it will lead to other questions where you would be forced to lie and as you can't lie, it is better to avoid it altogether.'

'Very sensible.' She smiled at a waiter offering a tray of canapés to them and helped herself to another tiny mouthful of something that resembled a miniature Yorkshire pudding stuffed with crab meat. It didn't even fill her mouth and he'd moved on to another guest before she could take another one. 'Are they going to serve any real food any time soon?' She was getting hungrier by the minute.

'It doesn't appear so,' Marcelo said in an undertone. 'There's a good restaurant a few streets away we can go to when it's polite to escape.'

'I'll try not to faint from hunger in the meantime.'

Ice-blue eyes captured hers. Amusement gleamed in them.

A frisson raced up her spine and she quickly looked away. She needed to keep her focus and not be distracted by Marcelo's gorgeous face and the crazy feelings looking at him evoked in her. She needed to be Princess Perfect for him.

Over the next hour that passed, though, Clara's composure start to flag. Holding herself straight the whole time and watching every word that came out of her mouth was exhausting, and so she was delighted when Marcelo spoke into her ear. 'Time to make our exit. Follow my lead.'

After a flurry of goodbyes and thank-yous, they left through a different door than they'd arrived.

The convoy of cars that had driven and accompanied them there were waiting for them.

'Can we walk to the restaurant?' she asked impulsively. If felt like she'd been cooped up all week and she had a real urge to breathe the evening air and see a bit of Ceres that wasn't castle.

He raised an eyebrow. 'In those shoes? Aren't your feet hurting you yet?'

She laughed. Until six days ago, Clara hadn't even owned a pair of high heels. 'They're killing me!'

'And you still want to walk?'

'If it's not too much hassle.'

She detected a moment's hesitation before he grinned and beckoned one of his guards over to relay the new instructions, and then they set off.

The Ceres capital's streets were how Clara had always pictured Rome, all narrow and lined with high renaissance buildings.

'How did I do?' she asked. 'I didn't insult anyone by mistake or embarrass you in any way, did I?'

'Not at all. They all thought you were charming.'

'Charming? Me? Ha! Still, that's good. I did try to behave like a princess.'

'Clara…' Marcelo shook his head. It had been an impressive effort on her part but it had pained him to see the effort she'd made, the fixed smile on her face. At times, her nails had dug into his palms but he doubted she'd even been aware of it. 'You did great, okay? You just need to relax a little and let the real you shine.'

'But people don't like the real me and I want your people to like me for your sake.'

There she went, in that matter-of-fact manner that took people aback at the first meeting of her, bluntly confiding that people didn't like her as if it were a simple fact of life.

'Of course people like you. *I* like you,' Marcelo told her, at a loss at what else he could say to refute her assertion. 'Alessia likes you.'

'It's okay, I wasn't fishing. Some people like me. Most don't. They find me too much. Oh, look, there's a caricaturist!'

They'd reached a piazza with a huge fountain in the centre, brimming with people eating and drinking the evening away in the plentiful restaurants and bars with outside seating. Following her gaze, Marcelo saw an artist speedily drawing a cartoonish portrait of a young woman striving to keep a straight face.

'You want one done?'

'I'd love to. But not right now. If I have to wait much longer for food I might start eating my own arm.'

'Then it's just as well we're nearly there.'

And just as well she'd refused, Marcelo thought with a stab of inward fury.

It was happening again, that impulse Clara brought out in him to say, 'To hell with decorum and duty.'

A prince of Ceres stopping at a caricaturist?

Eschewing his carefully laid out security detail to walk the city streets? They were hardly things that could be described as thrill-seeking, not in the way that part of him had been sated in his army years, but there was something about Clara that pulled those old, suppressed feelings out and made him yearn to throw caution to the wind and feel alive again. He could lie to himself that Clara's eyes when she'd asked if they could walk, which had had the same pleading quality Bob's got when begging for a treat, had been the reason he'd agreed but spending all this time with someone as honest as Clara forced a man to be honest with himself and the truth was he'd wanted to throw the shackles of his position aside too, even if only for a short walk.

The restaurant, a favourite of his family for its discretion and privacy, was busy but, as expected, the owner quickly found a table for them and another close by for his bodyguards, welcoming Marcelo with the subtle fawning he remembered from his visits here before.

'This is cool,' Clara enthused once they were seated at a small table for two, wine poured and their order taken.

'It has excellent food.'

'You've brought lots of women here?'

'Enough,' he answered drily. Marcelo was getting used to his fiancée asking the questions most other people were too frightened, wary or inhibited to ask. He liked that she could ask something like that without a hint of jealousy too. He liked that he didn't have to second-guess her.

'There's lots of women looking at you,' she observed. 'And I don't think it's just because you're a prince.'

He let his eyes soak up the beauty before him. 'I imagine there's a lot of men looking at you too, and I don't think it's because you're about to become a princess.'

She pulled a don't-care face. 'All the women kept staring at you at the embassy. I was worried I'd have to hit them with my bag if they started groping you.'

He burst into laughter. 'That really would be most unbecoming of a princess.'

She grinned. 'Then it's just as well I resisted.'

'Indeed.'

Clara leaned forward. The table was so small that if Marcelo were to lean forward too they could kiss. Lowering her voice, she said, 'Can I take my shoes off or would that be unbecoming?'

His eyes crinkled with amusement. 'Go ahead.'

Using her toes to work the heels, she slipped them off and stretched her aching feet. Straight away her toes prodded into male legs.

'Sorry.'

He smiled slowly. 'I'm not.'

Another of those dizzying rushes of heat flushed through her and, for a long, long moment, Clara's brain went entirely blank.

Luckily food arrived. Bread rolls and a plate of olives and cold meats were laid before them. Her stomach growling, Clara dived straight in.

This really was an excellent restaurant, she decided, all moody and dark. In the other corner a female singer was crooning songs as dark and moody as the décor. As it was in Italian, she didn't have a clue what she was singing about and decided she'd rather not know in case it was something inane. Instead, she jiggled her shoulders to the beat and enjoyed the feel of Marcelo's legs brushing against hers. There was nothing accidental about it now, and she enjoyed the thick, swirling sensation that coursed through her because of it. She hoped to enjoy more of this sensation later. Hoped a lot. But, of course, that was all dependent on Marcelo.

She had to wait until they'd finished their first course before she could remove the list she'd written earlier from her clutch bag.

'What's that?' he asked.

'A list of questions for you.'

'Questions about what?'

'Sex.' She waited until he'd finished choking before elaborating. 'I did like I said I would and had a good think about whether I want us to take things further, and I really, really do, but there are things we need to discuss first, so I wrote it all down so I wouldn't forget anything.'

As he looked a little dazed and was blinking more than was normal, she thought it best to add, 'That's if you still want something physical to happen between us?'

He took one long last blink, straightened, drank half the wine in his glass then fixed his stare back on her. His lips curved into a half-smile. 'Yes, *bella*, I want that very much.'

'I like you calling me that.'

'Bella?'

She nodded. Every time he called her it, a warm glow fizzed inside her.

'It suits you.'

'Thank you. So, can we go through my list?'

He took a deep breath, obviously bracing himself, then inclined his head. 'Go ahead.'

'Does sex hurt the first time or is that an urban myth?'

There was a flickering in his eyes. 'It doesn't hurt men but it's different for women. I think it can be uncomfortable the first time but, from what I understand, so long as you're relaxed and ready, the discomfort is fleeting.'

'How will I know if I'm ready?'

'Your body will tell you.'

'How?'

'Trust me, you'll know.'

Unconvinced at this assertion, Clara looked at her list for the next question. 'What if we get naked and I decide I want to stop?'

'Then we stop.'

'Have you had sex with a virgin before?'

'No.'

She shot her stare back to him. 'But you're sure you'll know if I'm ready?'

'No, *bella*, *you* will know.'

Still unconvinced, she said, 'Do you promise?'

'I promise.'

Hmm. She supposed time would tell. If it got that far.

'What was your first time like?'

'Over much too quickly,' he deadpanned.

She sniggered. 'How do you know if it's over too quickly?'

'As a rule, if the man comes before the woman, then it's over too quickly.'

She opened her mouth to ask her next question but before she could speak, their waiter returned to the table.

Marcelo exhaled slowly, glad of the reprieve the arrival of their main course brought.

Never in his life had he had a conversation like it. Strangely, there was something erotic about the businesslike manner Clara approached the subject.

And there was a lot erotic about the way she

happily, unashamedly devoured her risotto. The stirrings he'd been battling in his loins refired. Idly, he wondered if she would have the same enthusiastic appetite in the bedroom.

As if she could read his mind, once she'd cleared most of her bowl she went straight back on topic. 'If I have sex with you and I don't like it, will you expect me to have sex with you again?'

'No.'

'What if we're actually having sex and I don't like it and ask you to stop?'

'Then I would stop.'

'Has that happened to you before?'

'No.'

'Would your ego be bruised?'

'Probably.'

'Would you hate me for it?'

'I would hope not.'

She considered this then nodded. 'I wouldn't hate you if you decided you didn't like having sex with me. If we have sex, will it change the dynamic of our relationship?'

'Probably.'

'For good or bad?'

'I don't know.'

'So it would be a risk? I'm just thinking that we're going to spend the next year living together so we have to weigh up whether having sex is worth the risk.'

'Every action we take in life involves a degree of risk.'

'But we have evolved to mitigate most risks. We wear seat belts in cars, helmets on motorbikes... Do you wear condoms?'

'Always.'

'Do you have condoms?'

'Yes.'

'Sensible. If we get as far as having sex you'll have to wear one because, for obvious reasons, I've never taken contraception.' She finished her wine then topped both their glasses up. 'So, what do you think? Do you still want to have sex with me after all that?'

He gazed into the dark brown eyes and thought a man could sink into them and never come back up for air. 'More than I have ever wanted anything. And you? Are you willing to take the risk too?'

'Oh, yes...so long as you accept that I might change my mind halfway through.' She shrugged apologetically. 'I don't know how I will feel when we're naked and doing stuff so I can't promise anything.'

'Everyone has a right to change their minds.'

'So you accept that I might change my mind?'

'I will accept whatever you're willing to give.'

'Then shall we go home and possibly have sex?'

He arched a brow. 'Now?'

She looked at their almost empty plates. 'Unless you want dessert?'

Marcelo laughed through the pain of desire firing through him. 'As much as I long to whisk you back to the castle right now, we need to wait a few minutes or my obvious arousal will be front-page news.'

Her beguiling eyes widened. 'You're aroused right now? *Really?*'

He covered her hand with his and brought it to his mouth. 'Did you really expect me to have an hour-long discussion about sex with the sexiest woman on the planet and for my body not to react?'

Her eyes gleamed. 'I have a lot to learn.'

Now that she'd made her mind up Clara was impatient to get home but the short drive back to the castle, her hand tightly entwined with Marcelo's, dragged interminably. She remembered going on a school trip to a theme park when she was ten. She'd never been to a theme park before and had longed to ride on a roller-coaster. The night before, she'd been far too excited to sleep and had almost thrown her breakfast up before she left. That was the closest she could remember to how she felt now.

The thuds of her heart accelerated when their driver entered the castle's grounds. So powerful were they that their ripples churned in her belly. But there was no fear that she would be sick from them.

How funny that she'd lived twenty-two years without even a flicker of desire for a man and then, virtually overnight, her mind had become consumed with thoughts of Marcelo and sex. Now it was like those thoughts had fed into her bloodstream and spread to every nerve ending. Anticipation thrummed so heavily in her that her only fear was that she wouldn't like it when he touched her. She hoped she would like it and that all these wonderful new sensations had some meaning, otherwise why would she have them? It would be a disappointing waste.

They'd reached their private carpark.

They were home.

Suddenly anxious, she tugged at his hand. 'Promise you won't be angry with me if I change my mind.'

Through the castle grounds night lights, she saw his features contort.

Brushing a thumb along her cheekbone, he quietly said, 'I will take whatever you're willing to give. Nothing more. You have my word.'

The driver opened the door.

Clara gazed into Marcelo's steadfast stare a moment longer then smiled her relief and twisted round to jump out.

While she waited for him to join her, she gazed up at the stars and hugged herself. Whatever the outcome of what they were about to share together, she knew she was in safe hands and that when she got cold feet or found what they were doing too repulsive to continue, he would put his clothes back on and wish her a goodnight.

The odds were, it would be rubbish—how could reality live up to expectation, even if her expectations were low?—but at least when she eventually morphed into a white-haired spinster with a menagerie of pets, she'd be able to look back on this night and say she'd had a go at sex. She doubted they would go as far as full-blown sex because she had no idea how she was supposed to know when she'd be ready and just because excitement threaded her insides did not mean it would be the same on the outside. She might find his touch on her naked flesh repellent. She hoped not. She hoped she would like it enough that at some point her body would flash a neon sign at her that said, *You're ready!*

Once inside and the staff dismissed for the night, Clara kicked her heels off while Marcelo headed to the bar and removed a bottle of Scotch and two glasses with a raised eyebrow in question.

'Why not?' she murmured, thinking for the hundredth time how sexy he looked in a tuxedo. She hoped he looked as sexy naked. She hoped it got that far.

He poured them both a glass.

Eyes locked together, they drank.

'Another?'

She shook her head and pressed her palm to his cheek so she could feel the soft bristles of his beard on her skin. 'Let's go upstairs.'

He captured her hand before she could remove it. His stare bore into her with its intensity. 'Nothing more than you are willing to give.'

She smiled. 'And nothing more than *you're* willing to give.'

He laughed. It sounded pained to her ears.

At the top of the stairs, Marcelo opened his bedroom door and extended an arm in invitation. The expression on his face clearly told her he wouldn't argue if she changed her mind and locked herself in her own room.

She wasn't even close to changing her mind. At least, not yet…

CHAPTER NINE

CLARA HADN'T BEEN in Marcelo's room before. Her first impression was that it was very big and very masculine. There was no second impression because her attention was completely captured by the humungous bed. She headed straight to it and lightly stroked the black sheets.

Not hearing any movement, she turned and found Marcelo propped against the closed door watching her.

She soaked him in, her prince of a man. Could he see the thuds of her heart through her skin or hear the beats raging so loudly in her head?

He straightened.

Her breath quickened.

For the better part of the evening Marcelo had been fighting arousal. Clara's presence alone was enough to turn him on but their long conversation about sex had pushed him over the edge and for the first time in his adult life he'd been visibly aroused in a public setting. The drive home had consisted of him staring straight ahead and trying to keep a lid on his consuming awareness of the woman attached to the hand that had gripped his so tightly, knowing that when they reached the castle, Clara was trusting him to back off if she gave the word.

But now he was here, in his bedroom, facing her, the moment his body had been aching for finally at hand, and he, the man who'd always enjoyed sex for sex's sake, found he had cold feet.

This was all too clinical, something he would likely have celebrated with all his other lovers as it meant a guarantee of no awkward morning-after conversations but here, now, with Clara... It felt wrong.

He didn't know what he wanted but he did know that he didn't want clinical. Not with her.

Grabbing his hair, he opened his mouth to tell her this was a mistake and that the risk they'd discussed earlier was too great when she did something that stole the words from his tongue and the breath from his lungs.

She put her hands to her shoulders, pinched her sleeves and pulled them down to her waist.

All evening he'd tuned out the fact she was unlikely to be wearing a bra. Now he had proof of those suspicions.

Swallowing hard, his breath now back in sharp, ragged inhalations, Marcelo fought with all his might to halt the burn of desire roaring back to life inside him.

Her unflinching stare glued to him, she worked the dress's sash loose then moved her hands behind her back.

Seconds later, the dress fell to the floor.

Beneath it she was naked.

The thumps of his heart were violent enough to send blood pounding in his head.

She was more beautiful and ravishingly sexy than even his deepest fantasies had conjured, a Botticelli and nineteen-fifties bombshell combined together and brought to spectacular life. That she stood there without a hint of shyness when he knew he was the first man to have seen her naked only added to the effect.

She gazed at him a moment longer then stepped out of the red velvet puddle of her dress and walked towards him. There was no hesitancy in her steps.

It was only when she stopped before him that he noticed the colour high on her cheeks and the staccato of her chest as she fought the same battle for breath he was fighting.

The hint of a smile formed. She reached for his hand and lifted it, placing the palm at the top of her breasts. 'Can you feel my heartbeat?' she whispered.

It pulsed rapid and strong.

'Clara…' His intended protest turned into a groan when she gently lowered his hand to cover one of her breasts. It felt so full and yet so soft that the arousal he'd been battling enflamed him and he squeezed gently, reflexively. When he felt the nipple harden against his palm he had to smother another groan.

Her eyes widened. Darkened. She put a hand on his shoulder, lifted herself onto her toes and brought her face up to his.

Push her away. Tell her to get dressed. Leave the room. Do whatever you have to do to end this before it goes any...

Her hot breath danced over his lips. 'You smell wonderful.'

This had to *stop*.

Finally doing what he should already have done, Marcelo removed his hand from her breast, cupped her cheeks and looked Clara square in the eye, filled with resolve to end this now before it went any further.

But looking her in the eye was his biggest mistake he could have made because everything contained in them, everything she was feeling, was there for the reading. Desire. Curiosity. Wonder.

But no fear.

His groan escaped his mouth before he could stop it and his hungry lips fused hard against hers.

Her response blew his mind, scorching him with a heat that melted the mental shackles binding him.

He couldn't fight a hunger this strong. Not when it felt this good, this primitive, this *essential*.

Clara sank into the hard, possessive kiss with a moan of pleasure, her lips parting as her senses were instantly overloaded with the dark, intoxicating taste and scent of Marcelo.

The sensations their earlier almost-kiss had evoked in her were *nothing* on this. Nothing.

Flames erupted inside her, licking her into a furnace and liquefying her, and it was all she could do to bite her fingers into his shoulders to hold herself upright and sink even deeper into the possessive demands of his mouth. Parting her lips in movement with his, she experienced an even greater shock of pleasure when his tongue swept against hers. Oh, heavens…

If Marcelo didn't have such a good hold of her, her knees would have given way.

'You're laughing?' he accused raggedly, rubbing his nose into her cheek as he speared his hands through her hair.

'You just made my knees go weak,' she scolded with a laugh that sounded like no laugh she'd ever made before.

She felt dizzy. Breathless. Unable to believe what was happening inside her, the pulsing ache at the apex of her thighs, the tightening of her skin to an almost unbearable sensitivity…

The pads of Marcelo's fingers pressed into her scalp before he gently fisted her hair to pull her head back. His eyes were as liquified as her bones, his voice a husky growl. 'Shall we lessen the danger by moving to the bed?'

'You've still got all your clothes on.'

He gave another of those laughs that sounded like it came from a place of pain. 'It might be safer to keep it that way.'

'But I want to see you.' It shocked her how badly she wanted to see him naked. That tantalising glimpse of his chest her first night there had plagued her thoughts ever since.

He kissed her again but this time there was none of that delicious movement…but it didn't matter, not when he inhaled so deeply, making her certain he was breathing in her scent.

Sliding his hands down her arms, sending the most incredible tingles racing through her, he threaded his fingers through hers and led her to the bed.

Clara was glad to lay down. It wasn't just her knees that felt weak. Her legs felt like they'd been injected with water and, struggling to catch her breath, she watched Marcelo rip off his black bow tie and undo the top button of his shirt before stretching out on the bed beside her.

Propping himself up on an elbow, he gazed down at her for the longest time, and smoothed a lock of her hair off her forehead.

A shiver of delight danced over quivering skin.

Her heart was racing so hard she could no longer feel the individual beats.

Marcelo placed the lightest of kisses to the succulent mouth.

The urge to rip his clothes off and lose himself in Clara's heavenliness was so strong that he was working harder than he'd ever done before at anything to keep his desire in check.

He'd never felt hunger like this before but, his promise to her lodged at the forefront of his mind, he vowed to control it. He must.

When she stroked the bristles of his beard, he closed his eyes. Her every touch sent darts of fire through him, and when she glided her hand down his throat, he clenched his jaw and breathed deeply.

How could a simple touch burn the way hers did?

One by one, she unbuttoned his shirt.

His eyes flew open when she pressed a hand flat against his naked chest.

She was still gazing at him with that same expression, the strangely touching combination of wonder and desire and curiosity.

Her lips curved. 'Your skin is so smooth.'

He traced a finger over her collarbone. 'Yours is soft.'

She trembled and took a long breath. Her breasts lifted with the motion. He yearned to taste them, to take those pale pink nipples in his mouth and...

The painful tightening in his loins sucked the air from him.

Clara lay back down, greedily watching Marcelo shrug his shirt off and revelling at the darkening of his eyes as he watched her stretch her body. She'd never imagined her skin could be so sensitive to a touch or that someone's touch could feed a need for more touches. She'd never imagined, either, that she could take such pleasure in looking at someone. If she were asked to select one man to be an example of masculine perfection, Marcelo would be top of a list of one.

His hands went to the band of his trousers and, his stare fixed tightly on her, undid it and pulled the zip down.

Jaw clenched, he pushed them along with his underwear down past his hips, releasing his erection. Clara's eyes widened.

That made him smile wryly and, divesting himself of the last of his clothes, he laid beside her and stroked her cheek.

'Remember, *bella*, you're in control here. We don't have to do anything you don't want. We can stop right now.'

'Marcelo...' For once it was a struggle to speak the words in her head. 'You make me feel all...' She shook her head and palmed his cheek. 'I'm not ready to stop.'

'Anytime it gets too much for you, you tell me.'

'I will but right now I think that if you don't kiss me again I might have to kill you.'

Swallowing hard through his laughter, he bowed his head and kissed her.

Oh, but it was so hard and yet so tender and so, so addictive.

Wrapping her arms around his neck, Clara scratched her nails into the soft bristles at the nape of his neck and closed her eyes as the sensory pleasure of Marcelo's mouth and tongue winding with hers infused her.

She kept her eyes shut when his mouth moved from hers and gently kissed its way down her neck…heavens, that felt wonderful, and she would have cried her disappointment when he left her neck if he hadn't cupped her breast at that moment and sent another gasp flying from her lips.

The first time he'd touched her breast the effect had been a surprising pleasure. This time the pleasure was heightened, and she became aware of heat bubbling deep within her. It had been building all the way back since their embrace hours ago, but now it was no longer some distant squirmy feel between her legs but a pulse beating hard, and when Marcelo's mouth closed over the tip of her breast, the pulse tightened and she instinctively arched into his mouth and clasped his head.

She'd definitely found the door to heaven, she dimly thought as, kneeling between her legs, he lavished all his attention on the parts of her she'd been excited about when they'd first developed because she'd thought they automatically made her a woman but had then promptly became just another part of her with no more sensitivity than her little finger.

How wrong she had been. This was the headiest form of bliss she could have imagined.

What she loved as much as the wonderful things he was doing to her with his mouth and tongue and hands was the pleasure he was clearly taking from it too, and when he dipped down lower to kiss her belly, she thrilled at the scorch on her skin, thrilled at every little caress, until he kissed lower still and she suddenly realised where he was headed. Instinctively pressing the top of her thighs together, she gave a startled, 'What are you *doing*?'

Marcelo stilled and squeezed his eyes shut before resting his chin on Clara's beautifully rounded stomach.

She'd raised her head from the pillow. Her face was flushed and there was a dazed sheen he'd never seen in her eyes before.

'Do you want me to stop?' he asked huskily.

'Yes... No... Were you going to kiss me *there*?'

'Yes.'

'Why?'

Oh, his beautiful, confident, supersonically brained and yet utterly naïve fiancée.

'*Bella*, have you never brought yourself to orgasm before?'

Surprise flashed in her eyes. 'No.'

In that moment he felt such a wave of tenderness for her that it engulfed his heart. 'Then I want you to close your eyes and trust me when I say that kissing you there will give you nothing but pleasure.'

She still looked doubtful. 'Really?'

'Trust me. But you need to switch your brain off, close your eyes and feel. Don't think. Just feel.'

She stared at him a moment longer then rested her head back on the pillow. 'I trust you.'

Dio, that declaration engulfed his heart even stronger.

Clara took a deep breath and closed her eyes, and thought that maybe she shouldn't have skipped all the sex scenes on TV, and then she remembered that Marcelo had just told her not to think and—

She sucked in a breath as he gently parted her thighs and lowered himself further down the bed. The heat bubbling between her legs turned into a furnace as anticipation gripped her.

His tongue pressed into a spot that made her gasp and her eyes fly open.

What on earth…?

He pressed again at the same spot.

Oh…

Her thoughts turned into mush. And so did her body.

Closing her eyes, Clara sank into the unexpected but, oh, so incredible pleasure Marcelo was bestowing on her with his tongue, and when he moved a hand up to her waist, she grabbed hold of it and threaded her fingers tightly in his.

His tongue moved over and over the pulsating spot…and she moved with it, instinctively arching herself into his steadily rhythmic tongue to deepen the pleasure.

This was incredible. Oh, good heavens, she was on fire. The flames were suffusing her, throbbing and pulsing, building into something she could feel herself edging closer and closer to. Moans and gasps rang distantly in her ears… *Her* moans. Her gasps.

It was Marcelo's groan that sent her spiralling over the edge, and she cried out as spasms of unrelenting pleasure flooded her with a force that sent white light flickering behind her eyes and sent Clara soaring to paradise.

By the time the earth reclaimed her and she blinked her eyes open, Marcelo had climbed up her body. His gorgeous face hovered over hers. She'd never seen such wonder in his stare before. Or such unadulterated desire.

Her heart bloomed in gratitude for the unselfish pleasure he had just lavished on her, and she hooked an arm around his neck and lifted her head to kiss him, the shock of the musky taste on his tongue and the distant knowledge the taste was *her* diminishing as the flames deep inside her rekindled with fresh arousal. When she felt the stab of his erection against her inner thigh she was suddenly consumed with the need to feel him where the flames burned deepest. Inside her.

'Please,' she moaned, raining kisses over his face and wrapping her legs tightly around his waist and arching herself into him and trying to draw him into her. 'Please. I want this.'

Marcelo had no idea how he'd held on as long as he had.

Never in his life had he experienced as heady and erotic an experience as he had bringing Clara to orgasm with his tongue. Never had he known someone so responsive to his touch. And never had he been so responsive to another's touch. He was already close to coming himself and he'd had no gratification. Not of the physical kind.

There was a fever in his skin, his blood, his bones, all burning for her. The urge to give her what she was pleading for, to thrust himself into her slick heat…

In that moment he would gladly have a child

with this woman if it meant he could be inside her bare and feel every single part of their love-making without barrier.

Cupping her face, he kissed her hard, then pulled at her plump bottom lip with his teeth.

'Protection,' was all he could growl, and groped for his bedside table and the condoms in his top drawer.

Snatching the closest to hand, he ripped into the foil with his teeth and, still nestled between Clara's legs, twisted onto his side and deftly sheathed himself.

No sooner had he protected them than Clara's hungry, passionate mouth found his and she pulled him fully back on top of her, wrapping her arms around him as their tongues danced another heady duel and Marcelo positioned himself right where they both so desperately wanted him to be.

With Clara urging him on with her body and those soft moans that went straight to his loins, he gritted his teeth and inched his way slowly inside her, grasping at the last of his consciousness to remind himself that she was a virgin and…

She arched her bottom and thrust right back so they were fully fused together.

Wide, shocked eyes locked on his. A thump of dread that he'd hurt her spread through his chest.

Before he could get the breath to ask if she

was hurt, a wide smile of wonder lit her face and then her hot mouth was back on his and she was pressing every inch of her flesh into his flesh as if trying to fuse their skin together too.

That was the moment Marcelo lost himself completely.

Clara had never imagined it could be like this. This, making love with Marcelo, the feel of him inside her, the fusion of their bodies, the heat of his damp skin moving over her as he thrust in and out of her wildly, hands scrambling for flesh to hold onto, mouths biting…it was the most heavenly, thrilling feeling on this entire earth.

She didn't want it to end. She wanted this moment and all these beautiful sensations to last for ever. But she could no more stop the swell of release from building than she could stop the tides from turning, and when the spasms flooded through her, she clung desperately to him, crying out his name, holding onto the ecstasy for as long as she could, holding onto the thrills wracking her as Marcelo shouted out her name and bucked into her one last glorious time.

CHAPTER TEN

MARCELO'S HEARTBEATS WERE the heaviest he'd ever
known. They tremored through his bones and skin.

If the world had to end now he would leave
it gladly.

He could feel the strength of Clara's heartbeats through their conjoined bodies. He could
hear the raggedness of her breaths.

She held him as tightly as he held her and he
knew in his bones she didn't want to break the
spell binding them together any more than he did.

But no enchantment could hold for ever and,
as deeply reluctant as he was to move, he knew
his weight would soon crush her, and he gently
eased his face out of the crook of her neck and
lifted his weight from her.

Groins still locked together, he gazed down
at her face and into the dark brown eyes filled
with more of that wonder.

She swallowed hard. 'Well…that was something.'

He tried to speak, say something witty, but

his brain couldn't conjure anything and, even if it had, his mouth wouldn't cooperate.

So he kissed those delectable lips instead.

Her fingers scraped through his hair and then she sighed. And then she gave a flash of that mischievous grin he was coming to adore. 'Can we do that again?'

Laughing, he kissed her again. 'Soon,' he promised. 'Excuse me a moment—there is something I have to dispose of.'

Carefully withdrawing from her, Marcelo got off the bed and moved on surprisingly weak legs to the bathroom.

When he returned to the bedroom his heart lurched to find Clara gathering her dress from the floor.

'What are you doing?' he asked.

She smiled. 'Going to my room.'

'Why?'

Confusion drew her brows together. 'That's where my bed is.'

A lump formed in his throat. 'You can sleep here with me. If you want.'

She breathed in deeply, her lips pulling in and tightening into a straight line. 'Is that what you want?'

And then he saw it. The latent vulnerability.

Clara was preparing to leave his bed because she assumed that's what he wanted. She assumed he wanted her to leave because that's what she was used to. Rejection. It's what she protected herself from in her solitary life...

How many times could a woman break a man's heart?

'Yes. I want you to stay.'

Her smile as she dropped her dress broke his heart all over again.

Back under the sheets together, he gathered her into his arms.

'I've never slept in a bed with anyone before,' she confided. 'Apart from my mum. She'd let me sleep with her if I wasn't feeling well.'

He kissed the top her head and rubbed his nose into her silky hair.

'How many women have you slept with in here?'

He knew she wasn't talking specifically about sex. 'It isn't a competition.'

'I know. I'm just being nosy.' At least, Clara thought she was just being nosy.

She felt strange. Really strange. The beats of her heart were still erratic and there was a lethargy in her bones countered by a buzzing in her veins. But there was something else too, as unexpected as it was frightening because it reminded her a little of how she'd felt when she was a child and possessive of her mother. She had a vague memory of her Australian cousins coming to stay and one of them, Beth, grazing her knee and Clara's mum kissing the knee better. Clara, unused to sharing her mother's affection, had made sure to remind Beth that she was *her* mummy, not Beth's.

What she was feeling now was similar to that feeling and yet different. It came from a different place but she was at a loss to explain where that place was, and as she was at a loss she decided to push it from her mind and simply enjoy being held in Marcelo's arms.

Just lying there, being held so tenderly, his fingers making circles in her lower back...

It felt wonderful.

'Is sex always that amazing?' she asked.

He breathed deeply. 'No.'

Unsure if he was telling her the truth—after all, Marcelo had had sex with lots of women—Clara tilted her head back so she could see into his eyes.

As if he guessed why she was looking at him, he brushed his lips to hers and weaved his fingers through her hair. 'What you and I just shared, *bella*, that is not normal.'

'Really?'

'Really. What you made me feel...' He took another deep inhalation through his nose. 'I have never felt anything like that before.'

Well, that warmed her already impossibly warm insides up.

'I can't believe I was happy to go through life never experiencing that,' she said, fresh wonderment filling her. 'Do you think it would be like that with someone else for me? Or is it just because you're an amazing lover?'

He gave a choked laugh. 'I don't know. The chemistry between us is rare.'

'And you would know,' she agreed. 'And I suppose it's that chemistry that makes me want to do it all again.' Wriggling out of his hold, she raised herself up so she could study his face. 'What you did to me…is it nice if a woman does the same to you?'

He palmed one of her cheeks. 'Yes, but it's not something you should do because you feel you have to return a favour.'

'I think I would like giving you pleasure.' She encircled a brown nipple. 'I would definitely like to try.'

'You might like it more if I showered first.'

Her beaming smile shot straight into Marcelo's heart. 'Then let's take a shower together. I'm dying to see your bathroom.'

Deliciously spent from a second night of making love, Clara rested her chin on Marcelo's chest and tiptoed her fingers up and down his abdomen. 'Are you ever tempted to leave?' she asked idly.

There was a pause before he said, 'What, quit being royal?'

'It's been done before in other royal families.'

'What makes you ask?'

She laughed softly and pressed a kiss to his nipple. 'You rescued me because you were bored out of your mind. You're a man who thrives on adventure. Let's face it, there's not much excitement to be had as a working royal, not for a man like you.'

Marcelo stretched an arm above his head and fixed his gaze to the ceiling. 'There are days when I would like nothing more than to turn my back on it all but the damage to my family would be immense. Besides, this is the deal we made—they would support my military career and in return, when that career was over, I would become a full-time working royal. I'm living the life that's been mapped out for me since my birth and I shouldn't complain because it's a great life.'

'So you suppress yourself for your family's sake.'

'For duty's sake,' he corrected.

'But in your case, duty and family go hand in hand.'

'Sure,' he agreed. 'We are figureheads for our country. There are expectations about our behaviour. I got enough excitement in the army to last me a lifetime.'

'Obviously not or you'd have let your army friends rescue me,' she teased.

'That was one moment of madness that will never be repeated,' he said seriously.

'So you *are* suppressing yourself.'

'I have to.'

Pulling gently at the dark hairs on his chest, she said, 'If you really intend to stick to this life for the long-term then you need to find a way to channel your boredom. Otherwise you're just a caged tiger.'

'Better a caged tiger than a wild tiger causing more damage to the institution I was born in and the family I love.'

'I get that, but you need to find a way to take the edge off your boredom and accept your life as it is rather than fight it, or you're going to make yourself miserable. Look at me—I've lived on my own for six years. Sometimes I get a little lonely so I've learned to stave it off at the head with loud music or adrenaline-filled films or comedy TV shows. Plus I always have my dogs to cuddle up to. *Et voilà*, my loneliness is banished!'

Dio, he hated to think of her being lonely. Hated to think of her taking steps to mitigate the loneliness. Clara was too vibrant to live such a solitary life.

Before he could get his thoughts in order, she sat up and, with a flexibility that astounded him, straddled him. A spark of mischief flickered in her eyes. 'I know what will bring some excitement into your life.'

'Oh, yes?' He covered a breast and squeezed gently. 'And what's that?'

'Driving lessons.'

He groaned. 'That, I fear, will be too much excitement. And of the wrong kind.'

She grinned wickedly. Writhing lower, she licked his navel. 'Then let's see if I can give you some excitement of the right kind.'

Clara couldn't stop checking her make-up for smudges. She was minutes away from meeting her imminent in-laws and wanted to make a good first impression. It really mattered to her, which was why she'd insisted on getting ready in her own room rather than Marcelo's, where she'd spent most of the past week holed up. It was for his sake that she wanted the evening to go well. She imagined it would be awkward for him and make for an uncomfortable atmosphere if his parents hated her.

A knock on her door cut through the music blasting out.

'Come in,' she yelled, grabbing her phone to turn the volume down.

Marcelo strode into the room, freshly showered and dressed in a white shirt, navy waistcoat and charcoal trousers. One look was enough for her heart to catch in her throat and her pulses to accelerate.

It made her laugh to think she'd scorned those men in Marcelo's helicopter for taking seriously her words about women becoming nymphomaniacs once they'd had sex as she was seriously wondering if *she'd* turned into a nymphomaniac. Because sex was literally all she could think of. Sex with Marcelo.

Who'd have thought that she, Clara Sinclair, would fall head first into lust? It was the most delicious feeling, but also quite scary because there was no rationale behind it...unless you considered that Marcelo was the sexiest man to walk the planet and then it became the most rational thing on earth.

Which was why she'd insisted on getting ready on her own. She simply didn't trust herself not to get distracted by his gorgeous face and fabulous body.

Tonight, if only for a few hours, she was determined not to think about sex.

But only for a few hours. Sex with Marcelo was far too joyous to willingly deprive herself of it. Once they were married they'd have to take on official royal duties and have much less private time together, so she figured she might as well make the most of it while she could. He was clearly of the same mind, and she relished that this hunk of a man couldn't keep his hands off her.

'How are you getting on?' he asked, stepping over to her. 'Nearly ready?'

'I think so. As ready as I'll ever be. How do I look?' She'd selected a pair of blowsy muted yellow trousers, pairing them with a cream silk blouse with black polka dots and a matching silk scarf, topping the outfit off with a pair of the highest, most fabulous red heels she'd ever worn. With no beauty team to work their magic on her that night, she'd spent an age on her hair, twisting it into a side knot, then an even greater age on her make-up. She'd completed the look with a pair of diamond drop earrings.

He put his hands on her hips and studied her with that sensuous intensity she so adored. 'You look beautiful.'

She hastily pushed his hands away and stepped back. 'Please don't touch me or you'll make me want to have sex, but thank you. Do I look presentable enough for your parents?'

He folded his arms across his powerful chest and fixed her with a lascivious stare. 'You look good enough to eat, but if you mention wanting to have sex again I can't guarantee you'll still look presentable.'

Even his words were enough to make her insides clench in a heated throb. She took another step back. 'Please, don't. This is important to me.'

His stance softened. 'You sound nervous.'

'I *am* nervous. What if your parents don't like me?' Then she shrugged and answered her own question. 'I don't suppose it matters, does it? It's not as if they're going to be stuck with me for long.'

He breathed in deeply, a strange look forming in his eyes. 'I don't know how anyone could find you anything but adorable.'

Her heart made a skip. 'That's kind of you to say.' She took her own deep breath. 'Well, there's only one way to find out…'

Marcelo's parents, like his siblings, had their private quarters in the same part of the castle as his, but Clara had never been inside their domains. Mainly because she and Marcelo had barely left theirs. And also because, other than Alessia, they'd all been abroad.

The heels of her shoes clacked and echoed down the expansive corridors. Every person they met en route nodded politely—she could admit to feeling a little disappointed that commoners didn't have to curtsey or bow to family members; she'd have loved that!—and then they rounded a corner and were met with high double doors guarded by armed footmen.

The footmen nodded then stepped aside to admit them.

The moment they crossed the threshold, Clara's heart set off at a canter.

If the armed footmen hadn't been a giveaway that she was about to meet a monarch, what she walked into would have sang it loud and clear.

She'd thought Marcelo's quarters were rich and sumptuous?

They'd clearly entered a welcome room, and as she followed Marcelo through it, she craned her neck to take in the gold and cream papered walls, the gold wall lights, the gold and crystal chandeliers…and then they were walking through another vast area of deep blues and gold which in itself led to…

A much smaller room.

A much smaller, *cosier* room. But with the most extravagant furnishings she had ever seen…oh, how she coveted that yellow and gold chaise longue…and those gold and green drapes…ooh, and that bronze sculpture of the Madonna and Child…

And then they were in a dining room three times the size of Marcelo's, the table that could easily seat thirty people set for six in the centre; three either side…and the middle chair of the right-hand side wasn't a chair, it was a throne.

Terror grabbed her throat and, forgetting her vow not to touch him until the evening was over,

Clara instinctively grabbed Marcelo's arm and strained her face to his. 'Your parents are the King and Queen,' she hissed.

Bemusement spread over his handsome face. 'Funnily enough, I am aware of that.'

'No, silly. I mean, they're *royalty*. Proper bona fide royalty.' Seeing the bemusement turn to alarm, she tried to explain her incoherent thoughts as coherently as she could. 'Yes, I know they're royalty. I know you're royalty. But it's always felt quite abstract to me, a concept without any meaning behind it because to me you're just the really sexy, gorgeous man I'm going to marry for a while, and now it feels real and I'm about to meet a real king and queen and not just the people who are less than two weeks away from being my in-laws and what if I make a complete fool of myself and get the etiquette wrong and—'

A finger placed gently to her lips cut her panicked words off.

'*Bella*, breathe,' Marcelo ordered.

The large dark brown eyes blinked slowly. The slender shoulders rose slowly then fell.

He waited until certain she had control of her emotions then rubbed the back of his fingers against her soft cheekbone and quietly said, 'You have nothing to worry about. This is an informal family dinner—'

'Informal? That's a throne!'

'Trust me,' he soothed, wishing he could kiss her fears away but suspecting that to do so would only increase her panic as he would likely smudge her perfectly applied red lipstick. Fearing everything she'd learned in the princess lessons she so diligently sat through had flown out of her head in her anxiety, he told her what he thought she most needed to hear. 'This is informal. They're all looking forward to meeting you. You will be sat opposite me during the meal. If at any time you feel anxious, just look at me, and please, remember to breathe.'

The large eyes didn't flicker as she soaked his words in but then she blinked and gave a laughing shake of her head. 'That's useless advice considering that looking at you makes me unable to breathe properly. Seriously, man, wear a mask or something. Living with you is making my blood pressure go through the roof.'

At that moment, the double doors on the other side of the room opened and his parents entered, followed by his brother and sister.

The well-trained, unobtrusive staff filed in behind them and poured glasses of wine while Marcelo made the introductions.

By the end of her first glass, when they were all seated, Clara was feeling much more settled. Marcelo's family were human. What a relief!

As he'd promised, she was sat opposite him. She would have liked to have sat beside Alessia but his father, King Julius, sat between them, opposite Queen Isabella, who was as tiny as her daughter. The Queen was flanked by her two sons. Despite the size and grandeur of the room, there was an intimacy to the setting that Clara relaxed into, helped by the very real effort to be jolly and welcoming she suspected all the Berrutis were making, even the slightly frightening Amadeo. As the eldest sibling, he was next in line to inherit his mother's throne. She quite understood why Alessia had always referred to him as bossy.

Her new family were keen to know about her and peppered her with questions throughout their meal. What surprised Clara the most about the food was how homely it was, and she said so, adding, 'I imagined you would eat that posh stuff you get in the Michelin-starred restaurants.'

King Julius, who'd attended the same Scottish boarding school his sons attended and spoke fluent English the same as they did, burst into laughter. 'We have to suffer enough of that during our official engagements.'

Queen Isabella smiled. As a born princess, she'd been raised in this castle and taught by governesses. Her English was good but much more hesitant. 'You like it?'

'Very much,' Clara enthused. 'I prefer this to the posh stuff too.'

'I don't,' Alessia chimed in. 'Give me the posh stuff any day.'

'Are you still haunted by those atrocious meals they served at school?' Clara wanted to know.

Alessia shuddered. 'I still get nightmares. Don't you?'

'I still can't eat cabbage.'

'Did you enjoy your school days?' Amadeo asked over the laughter.

Now it was Clara's turn to shudder. 'God, no.'

Julius turned slightly to her, eyes alive with curiosity. 'Alessia tells us you were expelled. If you don't mind me asking, what was the reason?'

'Oh, I don't mind at all, but I wasn't technically expelled—I was asked to leave for setting off a fire alarm while there was an A-level maths exam on.'

'That *was* you!' Alessia exclaimed.

'Yes, but I didn't mean to do it. A bunch of us were mucking around outside the science block and I put my finger to the alarm as a joke and Kerry Buchanan pushed me and my finger went through it and set the alarm off. The whole school was evacuated and it mucked the exam up.'

'That sounds an extreme punishment for an accident,' Marcelo commented with a furrowed brow.

'Ha! They just used it as an excuse to get rid

of me, and the alarm was only a small part of it, really—I think me calling Miss Wilson a lying old hag played a part too.'

Alessia cackled with laughter. 'You didn't!'

'Well, she *was* a liar. She saw the whole thing and then lied and said I did it deliberately, and Kerry lied too and so did the others. They all lied.'

Clara smothered the pointless swell of anger remembering this event evoked. It was history and everything had been so much better for her since. Here, in this room, was her future and sitting across from her was the one person she was starting to believe she could rely on. Someone she adored. Someone she would miss when their time together came to an end...

'Why would a teacher lie?' Amadeo asked. Clara could hear the doubt in his voice. She understood it. People always doubted her.

'Teachers are as capable of lies and deceit as all other humans,' Marcelo answered for her.

Beaming at him, delighted that he was sticking up for her, Clara explained, 'She never liked me. I think it might have been from when I yawned in class and she asked if I was tired and I told her the truth that her voice was sending me to sleep. She had it in for me after that, was always marking me down and giving me detentions for any little thing.' She shrugged. 'She lied about the fire alarm incident, I called her a lying old hag, the head insisted I apologise, I refused so my brother was called in and advised to withdraw my enrolment from the school so I didn't have a permanent exclusion on my record. And that was that. My education over.'

A long silence followed.

It was Alessia who broke it.

'I can't believe they treated you like that,' she said, now sounding distressed. 'And over a fire alarm when other girls did so much worse and got away with it. That's not fair.'

Clara leaned across the King to pat Alessia's arm. 'Don't upset yourself. I was glad to leave that place. I hated it there. I've been much happier since I left.'

Who wouldn't be happy surrounded by dogs and cats and gerbils and all the other pets deemed too troublesome for their owners to care for them any longer? To Clara, those unwanted animals were her kindred spirits. No one had wanted her since her mother died, but that was okay. It really was. She was happy on her own.

She had also, she had to admit, found happiness with Marcelo. A different kind of happiness, one that was thrilling and joyous, a period of her life she would look back on with real fondness. But a period that had an end date to it. No doubt, by then, he would be happy to see her go.

'I'm so sorry for not calling you after it happened,' Alessia said, sounding close to tears. 'I should have done. I was a terrible friend.'

Her distress was so obvious that Clara left her seat to embrace her. 'Don't be sorry. You were a vacuous, vain, self-centred teenager like the rest of the horrid girls who went to that school, but you were always kind to me. If they hadn't forced you into having me as your roommate I would have run away long before I was expelled. You made that last year bearable for me.'

Alessia disentangled herself from the hug to fix tear-filled eyes on her. 'Was that a compliment or an insult?'

'Definitely a compliment. You couldn't help being a product of your environment.'

'You managed not to be.'

'Yes, and that's why I only had one friend. Now stop crying—you're getting tears in your lovely food.'

CHAPTER ELEVEN

MARCELO COULD NO longer taste his food. Even if he could taste it, he'd lost his appetite. The conversation surrounding him rang distantly in his ears. Apart from when Clara spoke. He heard her every utterance with crystal-clear clarity.

And there she sat, happily eating her dessert and drinking her wine and conversing and laughing as if what she'd relayed had had no bearing on her life. As if that incident hadn't stolen her future from her. Because she'd never attended another school. Never undertaken any of the exams that hold the key to having a life without limitation. She'd described the flat she lived in that came with her job. It was half the size of this dining room.

How could she be happy about any of that? How could she not be filled with anger and bitterness at everything that had been stolen from her?

How could she sit there, erupting with laughter with Alessia as they tried to explain the funky chicken dance they used to do for fun in their boarding school bedroom to his bemused mother?

These were thoughts still going round and round in his head when they wished his family goodnight.

'Well?' Clara asked the moment the guarded doors closed behind them, slipping her hand in his. 'How did I do?'

He swallowed back the bile that had been lodged in his throat since her narration. 'Very well.'

'Did they like me?'

'Judging by their body language, yes.' But he'd seen the private looks exchanged between his parents. As he'd suspected, his family had all been taken with Clara and her fresh, unfiltered view of her world. But those same characteristics also gave them doubts. From the way Amadeo kept trying to catch his eye, his brother's doubts were grave.

Marcelo had warned them that marrying Clara into the family was a gamble, but when the alternative was a diplomatic war, they'd collectively agreed it was a gamble worth taking. They had no right to complain if it turned out to be a gamble they might be on the losing side of.

As far as Marcelo was concerned, their doubts were unfounded. They hadn't seen now hard Clara worked in her lessons. They didn't know how determined she was to get things right. As long as she performed like a princess in public they had no cause for complaint. Damn it, she was only taking the role as a favour to them.

Aware anger was rising in him over things that hadn't been said or even alluded to, aware that it was a deep protectiveness of Clara making him want to slay dragons on her behalf, Marcelo expelled a long breath and tried to expel the misplaced anger with it. The dragon he wanted to slay wasn't his family but her brother.

When they reached their private quarters, Bob set himself straight on them. After fuss from them both, he made himself comfortable on his favourite sleeping spot: Marcelo's seventeenth-century armchair.

And then Clara set herself on him.

Throwing her arms around his neck, she rose onto her toes. She would have kissed him if he hadn't moved his face out of the way.

Her face clouded. 'What's wrong?'

Removing her hands from his neck, Marcelo clenched his jaw and breathed in deeply. 'What you were saying about your expulsion…'

'What about it?'

'I keep thinking about your brother. He shouldn't have accepted it. He should have fought on your behalf.'

'You must be joking. He fully supported the school's decision.'

'Did he kick you out of your home because of it? Is that why you started working at the shelter at sixteen?'

'Not at all—I got the job off my own back. Legally, he was supposed to look after me until I was eighteen but I'd had enough of school and being surrounded by humans who hated me so I decided to get a job where I was surrounded by animals instead. They're much nicer creatures and they never tell lies. And I was so lucky that the job came with accommodation. Andrew was delighted to be rid of me, though I'm quite sure he'd been looking forward to me turning eighteen so he could help me pack my bags and see me out of the door.'

'Why didn't your father make provisions for you?' Marcelo was aware his voice had risen to match the anger rising back up in him.

'Because he was an idiot who thought the sun shone out of Andrew's backside. The family wealth has been passed down to the eldest child for generations and the unspoken deal has always been for that child to look out for their siblings but my father always refused to see how much Andrew hated me. I'd have much preferred to have been sent to Australia to live with my mum's sister, but hey ho, I was stuck with Andrew. He did what was legally required and that was it.'

'How can you be so calm about this? You could be discussing the weather!'

'Why are you so angry?' she asked.

'Why aren't *you* angry?'

'I have nothing to be angry about.'

'You have *everything* to be angry about. *Dio*, Clara, all your life, the people who should have protected you treated you—'

'Being angry doesn't change anything,' she interrupted. 'It's done. Andrew will join our father in hell for how he's treated me over the years plus he's not getting an invite to our wedding so the whole world will know we're estranged and that we've snubbed him—trust me, that's social death to him. I was always an embarrassment to that man. And I told you, I was happy to be expelled. I hated that place and that place hated me. No one wanted to be friends with me and I can't say I blame them,' she continued, barely pausing for breath. 'I was always getting the other girls into trouble. I didn't mean to but the teachers knew that if they asked me who'd been breaking whatever school rules had been broken and I knew who the culprit was then I'd tell them. I didn't want to and I never would have volunteered the information but if they asked me, what else could I do?'

'But I thought *you* were the troublemaker?'

'I was that too. Well, that's how they viewed me. I never meant any harm, unless you count bunking off the lessons I hated as harmful, but if a teacher saw me yawning and asked if I was bored when I was bored then what was I supposed to say other than yes? And why was organising a petition to employ people who can actually cook rather than serving cold food that's so overcooked the nutrients are long dead and buried considered troublemaking, or picketing for the heating to come on earlier in the mornings so we didn't turn into icicles when getting dressed? And why was pointing out to a maths teacher that there's a simpler way to formulate an equation considered troublemaking?'

Pulling her back to him and wrapping his arms tightly around her, he rested his cheek against her silky hair and tried to get a grip on the tempest of emotions flooding him.

'Teachers are never keen to have students challenge their authority,' he muttered.

With the strong beat of Marcelo's heart thumping beneath her ear, Clara sighed. For a moment her indignancy relating her hated school days had come close to bubbling into something darker.

It disturbed her how often she'd found herself squashing the darker emotions of her past since she'd been in Ceres. Maybe it was because she'd so stupidly allowed herself to believe that Andrew's request that she travel to Monte Cleure on his behalf meant he finally wanted to put the past behind them and let her be a sister to him. Or maybe it was because relating it all to Marcelo brought it all back and made it feel more present than it had in a long time.

'Thank you,' she said.

'For what?'

'Sticking up for me earlier. For being angry on my behalf even if it is pointless. It means a lot.' It meant more than she could ever express. No one had ever stuck up for her before. Not since her mother. Having someone on her side felt truly special, and she would hold onto it for as long as it lasted.

He gave a muted laugh and pressed his lips to the top of her head.

'Have you stopped being angry now?' she asked.

'I'm trying.'

'Try harder.'

He gave a muted laugh and kissed the top of her head for the longest time. 'I don't think I will ever stop feeling angry about this. Your life could have been so different.'

'But my life is *good*. It's a happy life. I know not many people understand me or get me but I'm cool with that. Like when I told Alessia she was a product of her environment, well, I'm a product of mine. Losing my mum was the single most traumatic moment of my life. I didn't speak for three months after she died and then when I found my voice again it was shutting up that became my issue. It was like a filter had been ripped away not just from my voice but from my eyes and my impulse controls, and I can't always control it but I do try and while you and I are married I will try as hard as I can to remember my lessons and not embarrass you.'

He held her even tighter. 'You could never be an embarrassment to me. You're uniquely you. Never lose that.'

She pulled her head back to look up at him. Her eyes were shining but Marcelo detected a faint hint of disbelief. 'Do you mean that?'

'Yes. And I mean this too…' He swallowed hard. '*Bella*, when we say our vows, I want them to be real.'

As Marcelo spoke, a rush of relief flushed through him to finally put into words the feeling that had been growing inside him.

'But they will be real,' she said. 'I'm never going to get married again so I won't be telling any lies when we say them.'

'That's not what I mean.' He pressed his forehead to hers. 'I don't want our marriage to last for only a year. I don't want any end date.' If he had to marry, why not the woman he was having the best sex of his life with? And it wasn't just sex. Clara was a breath of fresh air in the staleness of his life—why let that go over an arbitrary cut-off date when he knew damn well he'd never meet anyone like her again? She might not be the perfect princess he was supposed to settle down and breed with, but she was the perfect woman for him.

She pulled her head back again, her eyes wide. 'Are you saying you want to marry me for real?'

'Yes.'

'Why?'

'Because you're the only woman who can make the mundane fun and I will never meet another you.'

She just stared at him.

'What do you say?' he asked into the silence.

She blinked and grazed her bottom lip. 'Can I think about it?'

A week later, just as the beauticians finished working their magic on Clara for the pre-wedding party, she received notification that Samson and Delilah were cleared to travel to Ceres. After firing messages back and forth, she was delighted when it was confirmed their journey's end would coincide with her and Marcelo's return from their honeymoon in the Seychelles. She'd have her family back again!

How lucky was she? She'd have her smart, gorgeous husband and three dogs under the same roof as her.

Hurrying into Marcelo's room to share the

good news, she found him fastening his ball and chain cufflinks. Inordinately pleased at this, she beamed before explaining everything.

'I'm getting my babies back!' she finished.

He raised an arched brow. 'Your babies?'

She hugged herself. 'That's how I think of them. I've known since I was a teenager that I won't have babies of my own, so my dogs take that baby space in my heart... Why are you looking at me like that?' There was the strangest expression on his face but she couldn't quite decipher it. 'Do you think I'm mad or something? I mean, it's fine if you do, but you already know I'm bats about my—'

'You're not mad, *bella*,' he interrupted softly. 'I was just thinking you will make a wonderful mother and wondering why you've never wanted any of your own.'

'Oh. Well, it's not that I don't want them but rather... Sorry, do you really think I'd be a good mum?'

He smiled but there was still a lingering of that strangeness. 'You'd be loving and protective. What more would a child need?'

'A father? I mean, that's why I never thought I'd have them. You need sperm to make a baby and as I never thought I'd have sex and the thought of using a turkey baster doesn't appeal...' Her words tailed off at the starkness of Marcelo's stare.

She swallowed, suddenly uncertain and suddenly a lot breathless. 'What?' she whispered.

'We could have children.'

Her hands flew to her chest. The thuds of her heart smashed against them. 'What?'

'You and me. You want children. I want children. If you agree to marry me for real then why not?'

In the week since she'd asked for time to think about his proposal, he hadn't mentioned it again. But it hung between them.

Clara was in a genuine flux about it. Her feelings for Marcelo ran deep but were those feelings only because of the sex? How was a girl supposed to know? Her life had been happy since she'd been expelled from that horrible school and she'd left home. She and her pooches all lived for the moment taking each day as it came.

She couldn't compare that happiness to what she had with Marcelo because it was so different.

Her happiness with Marcelo was off the charts but she couldn't help the whispers in the back of her mind that these feelings shouldn't be trusted.

'Do you really want to have children with *me*?'

His gorgeous face was steadfast. 'There is no

one else on this earth I would rather have children with.'

Thuds battered hard against her chest.

She could be a mum, she thought dazedly.

She could have children with him.

An image flashed in her mind. A fast forward of her life. Her and Marcelo with a small boy and girl, running through the castle vineyard, Samson, Delilah and Bob racing with them. Beaming smiles on the humans' faces. Wagging tails from the animals. Kisses. Hugs. Piggybacks.

Could that really be hers?

Could it?

Looming larger than life in the whole perfect picture was Marcelo. The man who'd brought the woman out of her.

He'd saved her life. That alone was enough for her to hold the deepest of affection for him. Marcelo would always have a piece of her heart and the whole of her gratitude.

She wanted to trust him with the rest of her heart, she realised as emotion swelled from deep inside her.

She wanted to trust the whole of herself to him.

Reaching for his hand, she threaded her fingers through his and stared into his piercing ice-blue eyes. His chest was barely moving. He was holding his breath, she realised.

She smiled. Looking at him always made her want to smile. 'If I was to have children with anyone, it would be you. Only you.'

His throat moved. After a long moment his mouth opened but a loud rap on the bedroom door interrupted the moment and in an instant the glow of emotion evaporated and was replaced by the same nerves she'd experienced just before she'd met Marcelo's parents.

Marcelo noticed the immediate change in Clara's demeanour. Fear rang large in her eyes and it crushed the urge to demand she put him out of his misery and tell him what she was thinking, about a real marriage and, now, about children. About having a family with him.

Now that he'd become accustomed to his own feelings on the matter, the thought of marriage and children: family, no longer made him want to run for the hills. Not when the wife and mother was Clara.

She'd kept him hanging for her answer for a week. Keenly aware of what she'd be giving up to be his wife for real, namely her future freedom, he'd vowed not to pressure her. He'd tried telling himself it would be no big deal if she turned him down—why would anyone voluntarily tie themselves to a royal institution in this day and age?—but the longer she'd kept him hanging, the tighter his guts had cramped.

But, he rued, even if they weren't about to be

the star attractions at a party filled with nobles, politicians and a smattering of celebrities, he couldn't force her to commit to something she was still unsure of. He knew it. He'd seen it in her eyes before the fear had taken over.

'You look stunning,' he said gently, taking her other hand and bringing it to his chest. And she really did, wearing an elegant cream halter-neck dress that swished softly to her ankles, her hair swept off her face in an equally elegant chignon. 'Every inch the princess.'

Her chest rose and fell raggedly and then the wide smile he'd come to adore so much beamed into his heart.

Squeezing his fingers, she said, 'Come on, my prince. Take me to the ball.'

Hands clasped together, they left their quarters.

As they took the long walk through the maze of wide corridors to the stateroom the party was being held in, Marcelo wondered if Clara's honesty had changed him in some way. When they'd first agreed to marry, he'd had no problems at all with making vows he didn't intend to keep. Now, all he could think was that he needed those vows to be true. From both of them.

The enormous duck-egg-blue and gold-coloured stateroom had been decorated with an abundance of silver and gold balloons and decorations that glittered under the clever party lighting. Although this party was being hosted for diplomatic purposes, another way of reinforcing to the world that Marcelo had swept Clara from the Monte Cleure palace out of love, royal officials had gone to great lengths to create the illusion of a real engagement party. Clara hadn't even thought of it as an engagement party until she saw the pile of presents carefully displayed on an antique table in the corner. In a week, she supposed there would be more presents for their actual wedding.

An hour into the party and Clara relaxed a fraction. What she found helped was reminding herself that all the people here were human just like her. Even the President. Even the King and Queen of Agon. Even the businessman currently believed to be the richest person on earth.

One thing she was particularly grateful for was the Queen taking her under her wing. Arm in arm, they circulated amongst the two-hundred-strong guests, introducing Clara properly and exchanging a few words before moving on.

And, as always, she was grateful for Marcelo. When the buffet opened—and it was a buffet like no other she'd ever had with its vast array of creative and colourful platters—she remembered the training she'd been given and ate dainty portions which, mercifully, he kept adding to for her.

Marcelo was a prince in every way.

Her prince.

The most exciting, unselfish lover a girl could wish for. Her personal cheerleader.

Her protector.

The man who suppressed such an intrinsic part of himself for duty and family. The reason she was so determined to master decorum and etiquette.

How could she possibly be torn about accepting the life he was offering, which was a whole life with him? A true lover. Children. A family. All the things she'd never allowed herself to want simply because it was akin to wanting smaller feet. Pointless.

And now Marcelo and the chance to create their own family was being dangled before her and she realised she *did* want it. She wanted it badly.

So why hadn't she already snatched his hand off for it?

Another hour passed. Somehow she, Marcelo and Amadeo had been drawn into a group of people whose names she didn't remember. Clara was careful to look interested, smile a lot and adopt the listening pose when anything was addressed directly to her. One woman brought up the topic of artificial intelligence and the next thing she knew a rabid discussion about the benefits as opposed to the dangers was under way.

'What's your opinion on the matter?' the most vociferous of the antis asked her.

Remembering the one thing that had been drummed into her over and over, namely never give an opinion on anything, she replied, 'Oh, don't ask me! I was expelled from school at sixteen and left without any qualifications.'

The originator of the subject's eyes widened before laughter rang out around their small grouping. Even Amadeo was smiling, but when Clara met his stare, there was something—a coldness—that sent unpleasant prickles up her spine.

Had she said the wrong thing?

She tried telling herself she'd imagined it, for every time their eyes met thereafter, there was nothing but the same warmth he gave everyone else, but she thought it wise to keep all talk to the minimum, and spent the next hour exhausting herself with the strength of her concentration.

'Relax, *bella*,' Marcelo whispered in her ear when they found themselves alone for the first time since the party started.

'I'm trying but it's so hard. I'm terrified of saying the wrong thing again.'

Before he could answer, Alessia joined them and swiped two glasses of the free-flowing champagne from a passing waitress. She handed one to Clara, who sipped at it. No way was she going to overindulge that night, not when she was fighting her motormouth with everything she possessed. It really didn't need any stimulus, thank you very much.

As the evening had worn on, the music from the professional DJ—deliberately chosen to project a youthful image to the world—had steadily increased, tempting more and more people onto the dance floor. Clara kept experiencing nostalgia pangs, remembering school nights when Alessia would put her music on in their room and they would dance madly...

As if her nostalgia had conjured it by magic, a song came on that immediately made Clara and Alessia look at each other. It was their funky chicken song.

Excitement rushed through her, transporting her back to that nostalgic time as if she were right there, right now, and, without thinking, Clara quickly knocked back her champagne, gave her empty glass to Marcelo with a cheeky grin, then dragged a protesting Alessia onto the dance floor.

'Come on, Princess Twinkletoes,' she laughed, 'You know what to do.'

CHAPTER TWELVE

'How did I do?' Clara asked nervously as she slipped her shoes off in the entrance hall of their quarters.

Marcelo removed his jacket and bow tie, taking in the flush of colour heightening her cheeks and the glow suffusing her. But there was uncertainty mingled in the happy glow.

He thought of her dancing with Alessia. The joy on her face as she'd flapped her arms and kicked her knees back and did that chicken thing with her neck, and encouraged Alessia to join in. How the whole dance floor had ended up joining in this spontaneous mad dance, the laughter on the dancers' and watchers' faces alike... with the exception of Amadeo. His brother had tried to hide it but he'd been angry at this lapse in decorum when there was a press corps in attendance.

He remembered too the flash of cold anger on his brother's face when Clara blithely brought up her expulsion.

Clara had seen that flash too. He was certain of it. He'd seen the way her features had crumpled in consternation before she'd picked herself back up again, but only to hold herself even more rigidly.

Knowing it would devastate her to think she might have caused embarrassment when she'd been so determined to be on her best behaviour for them, he put his hands on her hips and pulled her to him. 'To me, you're perfect.'

It might not be an answer to the question she'd asked but it was a truth. And it was a truth that smoothed away the uncertainty and made her chest rise sharply. A dreamy smile lit her beautiful face as she clasped his hands and tugged him into the living room.

Skipping away from him, she put her bag on a table and pulled out her phone. A moment later, music filled the room.

It was one of the love songs she so loved to listen to.

Her eyes locked back on his and the dreamy smile returned. Stepping to him, she put a hand to his chest. 'Dance with me.'

Putting his hands back to her hips, he slid them around her waist as her hands slid up his chest and around his neck.

Eyes locked together, they began to sway to the music.

The tune changed. Another love song came on. This one had a more sensuous vibe.

The dreamy smile had faded but its echoes rang vividly in her eyes. 'This song makes me think of you,' she whispered. Her thigh slipped between his.

Their lips brushed together. They continued to sway.

He untied the neck of her dress. Her hips continued to sway as he pulled the zipper down to her bottom. The dress swayed in time to the floor.

She arched her neck, inviting his kiss. And then he kissed the swell of her breasts before sliding a hand around her back to unclasp her strapless lacy bra. It was the red one he'd seen in its box when he'd still been foolish enough to think he could resist Clara's erotic chemistry.

Her fingers skimmed over his throat to the top button of his shirt. When she'd finished unbuttoning them, she spread the shirt apart and pressed the tips of her naked breasts to his chest. Her breaths were slowing and becoming more ragged against his mouth. Desire saturated her stare.

Working simultaneously, still swaying, lips still brushing together, they undid Marcelo's trousers and pushed them down with his remaining scraps of clothing. Clara's knickers followed. Not breaking the connection between them, they stepped out of the discarded items. His erection jutted into her abdomen. She moaned.

He clasped her bottom and kissed her deeply. Passionately. She wound her arms around his neck and raised a thigh, rubbing herself against him.

Groaning, Marcelo lifted her into his arms and carried her to the nearest wall. Lithely, she wrapped her legs around his waist and held herself tightly to him.

Dio, he wanted so badly to be inside her, but there was a growing whisper in his head reminding him he needed to get protection…

As if she could read his thoughts, she dug her fingers into his skull and looked him deep in the eyes.

'I want to feel everything,' she whispered.

He stilled. Breathing heavily, he tried to read the desire-saturated eyes.

'Make love to me, Marcelo. Be my husband for ever.'

As Clara uttered the words, a sense of rightness filled her that was as powerful as her hunger for Marcelo's possession, and then he thrust into her and his naked possession was so all-consuming that her thoughts spilled away and all she could do was lose herself in this most glorious and heady of rides as he drove into her over and over, taking her to a peak that convulsed her entire body until he slammed into her one last time, roaring her name.

Marcelo thought he must have died and gone to heaven.

Clara was riding him. Her hands were on his shoulders, the tip of a breast in his mouth as he lavished it with the attention that always fed her arousal.

Dio, he loved her breathy moans. Loved the way she rode him with such abandon. Loved the exquisite feel of being bare inside her slick tightness… *Dio*, he didn't think he could ever get enough of that feeling.

And he loved her.

He'd known it since the impulse to punch his brother in the mouth for that flash of cold anger at Clara's mad dancing had found him clenching his fists and then avoiding him for the rest of the evening lest he give in to it.

Her moans deepened. Her fingers bit deeper into his flesh.

Dio, he loved her. He wanted her, wanted this, for the rest of his life.

She was his.

And he was hers.

Sensing Clara was nearing her peak, he gripped her hip as she threw her head back, her hair falling like a waterfall. She stiffened and ground down and then the spasms tightened around him and pulled him deeper inside her, so deep that Marcelo let himself go with the mindless abandonment he'd never allowed himself before.

Two days later, Marcelo waited until his family were seated before launching into the speech he'd mentally prepared. 'We need to delay Clara becoming a full-time working royal. I know this will add pressure to your workloads, but I need our engagements to be closed house for the immediate future.' His and Clara's royal diaries were already filling with engagements. They were due to hit the ground running as soon as they returned from their honeymoon. 'Clara and I have decided our marriage is going to be permanent, and that is why I've made this decision. She's going to be a permanent member of our family and I need her to be comfortable and happy in the role she plays in it, and she's—'

Amadeo rose from his chair, his face taut with anger. 'Are you trying to ruin us? We can mask her inadequacies for a year but for *life*?'

'If you could see past your own snobbery you'd see Clara has the potential to be the greatest asset this family ever had.'

'Never.'

Marcelo spread his hands flat on the table and leaned forward. 'Did you not see everyone's reaction to her last night when she was dancing?

How they responded to her? She's a breath of fresh air. Our people will love her, but for now she needs more time and space to adjust to this life, and to learn to relax into it. I will not have her feeling that she can't breathe when we're working, when this is going to be her life for the rest of her life. I will not have her feeling that she's not good enough when she *is* good enough. She just needs to believe it in herself.'

He was met with silence.

'Let me make this clear. Clara is going to be one of us for good and you all need to learn to accept this if you want me to stay a part of this family.'

'Don't say such things,' his mother said, visibly upset.

'Then give me your support. Give Clara your support.'

'Of course we'll support—'

'How can you ask us to support you in a marriage that might see you taking a back seat from most of your duties indefinitely?' Amadeo demanded, interrupting their mother.

'If the doctors hadn't saved my life, I would have taken a back seat from all of my duties permanently,' he reminded him icily. 'Clara is determined to be an asset to this family. With help and support she can do it, but, and I reiterate this, it will take time. She is the only woman who will make marriage tolerable for me so if you want me to live up to your expectations and breed the next generation it will be with her or no one. Now, do I have your blessing or not?'

'You have mine,' Alessia said with a rueful smile. 'And I agree with your reasoning. Anything I can do to help, just let me know. Congratulations by the way.'

One by one, the others, even a reluctant Amadeo, gave their blessings too.

'Thank you,' Marcelo said. 'One last thing—I would appreciate if this discussion stays within these walls until after our honeymoon. Clara doesn't need to know about this meeting or the reduced number of engagements. She's had no involvement in setting them up. I will not have her hurt for anything.'

Clara couldn't stop smiling. So utterly delicious did she feel that for the first time in possibly her whole life she wished she had a friend she could share these feelings with. Alessia couldn't count because she didn't think Alessia would appreciate Clara raving about what a wonderful lover her brother was and how making love to him without protection had brought a whole new closeness to them. Of course, it wasn't the act itself as the meaning behind it, but it all merged together and represented the same thing. They'd committed themselves to each other. Their marriage would be real. They would have a family.

Oh, she could hug herself.

A real family? *Her?*

And soon she would have Samson and Delilah with her too. Her life really would be complete!

Needing to let the joy out, she did three cartwheels in a row. Bob, who she was currently training to walk off-lead in the field off the back of their private garden, found this very exciting and ran around in circles to show his admiration. She wondered if she should bow for the castle's security team, who would no doubt be observing her from their monitors. Their private quarters were private and that included their garden. Everything else was under surveillance.

Marcelo was worth the intrusion she one day hoped to become used to.

Her phone beeped. Indicating first for Bob to sit, she pulled it out of her back pocket. Her good mood plummeted.

It was her brother. How he had her new number she didn't know and figured it was probably best she never did know as she might have to kill the person who'd given it to him.

Gritting her teeth, she read:

Hope the wedding preparations are going well. Wondering if you can check with the organisers as my invitation seems to have got lost in the post. Alison and Johan have received theirs and are en route to Europe.

Oh, that cheered her right up. Alison was her mother's sister, the aunt who lived in Australia. She imagined Alison and Johan's delight in confirming to Andrew that they'd received the golden ticket he so obviously craved.

What an arrogant plonker that man was. To think she'd once longed for his approval! She didn't need his approval any more. She didn't need or want anything from him. If she didn't have Marcelo and his family's reputation to think of, she'd sell her story to the press and shame Andrew to the whole world. Still, this was just as good a shaming incident. No way the British press would let Andrew Sinclair's failure to attend the wedding of the year go unreported.

Striding back to the castle, eager to share the message with Marcelo, she fired a message back that lifted her mood even more.

Oh, dear, that is a shame. Why don't you ask your good friend King Pig if you can be his plus one as I hear he's struggling to find a victim to take with him? Actually, no, scrap that as I think his invitation got lost in the post as well. Amazing how karma strikes, isn't it? Hope Florence and the kids are all well. Please tell her that if she ever sees sense and dumps your sorry ass, she'll be welcome here with open arms.

She pressed send as she stepped into the boot room and then blocked her brother's number so she never had to deal with him again.

Feeling lighter in her heart than she'd done in years, Clara removed her boots and wandered through their utility room. She gave a cheery good morning to one of the maids, and was about to head to Marcelo's offices, where he was tied up in meetings, when she spotted the tall man sat reading a newspaper at the round corner table in the living room.

'Hello,' she said, surprised to see Amadeo. 'Are you waiting for Marcelo? He's in meetings with—'

'I have just left him,' he said, cutting her off and rising to his feet with stiff awkwardness. 'I am here to see you. Please, take a seat.'

The maid poured them both a coffee before Amadeo dismissed her with an imperious flick of his head.

'Clara...' Amadeo sighed. 'It will make it easier for both of us if I can speak freely.'

'I appreciate honesty, so go ahead.'

He nodded. 'I thought as much. Before I go any further, I want you to know that none of this is personal. I have no wish to hurt your feelings, but I am concerned your behaviour could bring harm to my family.'

An icy shard sliced through her chest. 'Is this about my dancing?'

'You didn't just dance the funky chicken or whatever it's called the other night,' he continued with a touch of disdain. 'You told the world that you were expelled from school.'

'I didn't tell the world. I told the people in our group.'

'All of whom have few scruples when it comes to sharing gossip. Which is what your expulsion now is. Gossip. It won't be long until the press hear about it. They might already know—enough of them were in attendance that night.'

'Photojournalists,' she felt compelled to remind him.

'The clue is in the journalist part. Have no illusions, they will hear about it and when they do it will be open season. We have no control over what the press chooses to print or what our people think. What concerns me is that you're a loose cannon who will unwittingly give the press even more fodder.'

She lifted her chin defiantly. 'I have nothing to hide.'

'We all have things we wish to keep private.'

'I don't. In any case, they would have heard about the expulsion at some point.'

'Possibly. The fact is, we'll never know because you kindly fed it to them yourself.'

'Do you want to cancel the wedding?' she asked bluntly over the ice now infecting her entire body.

'It's too late for that,' he replied with equal bluntness. 'And as it is going to be very difficult for everyone if we have to spend the next year doing damage limitation whenever you're incapable of knowing when not to speak, we've agreed that all your future engagements will be of the closed-house kind like the one you attended at the embassy, and all other scheduled engagements are to be given to other members of the family. This will leave you with very few engagements and so greatly reduce the potential risks for embarrassment.'

Cheeks burning with humiliation, Clara looked him straight in the eye. 'This doesn't just concern me, it concerns Marcelo. Have you spoken to him about this?'

'These measures are his idea.'

Her stomach plunged like she'd fallen through a trapdoor. 'You what?'

'He called a family conference about it earlier.'

Bile filled her throat again and smothered her taste buds. She had no idea how she was able to talk through it. 'And did he agree to you being the one to tell me?'

'No. He requested you not be told.'

'So why *are* you telling me?'

'Upon reflection, I decided you deserved to know. Walls have ears, even castle walls—I didn't want you to hear about it through exaggerated whispers. I thought it best to talk directly to you so you understand why we are taking these measures and to reiterate that this isn't personal.'

She jutted her chin. 'It feels personal.'

He raised a shoulder in apology. 'We are indebted to you for agreeing to marry Marcelo and sparing us a diplomatic war with Monte Cleure, but you yourself observed early on that you're not princess material.'

Taking a deep breath, she looked him straight in the eye. 'Then you must be relieved I'm only going to be a part of your family for a year.'

It was the flicker in his eye that gave him away and, in one fell swoop, everything became clear.

Amadeo had sought her out not to chastise her but to warn her off his brother. He didn't want her to be a permanent member of his family. This was his way of telling her she had to stick to the one year of marriage as had been originally agreed.

Rising to his feet, he said, 'We *are* indebted to you, Clara, and we want your year with us to be as happy and as comfortable as it can.'

'As long as it's far from the public eye and only for one year?'

He gave a faint smile. 'Marcelo said you had a quick brain. I thank you for your understanding.'

She waited until he was about to leave the room before calling his name. 'Amadeo?'

He turned back to her.

She summoned her brightest smile. 'Has anyone ever told you that you're a pompous ass?'

Marcelo swam harder than he'd ever swum before. Length after length he drove his body, determined to work the guilt out before he returned to his quarters.

By the time he'd exhausted himself, his mind was clearer.

There was no need for guilt.

He wasn't lying to Clara by keeping the family conference from her. Their wedding was five days away and she was fizzing with excitement for it and their subsequent honeymoon. Why dampen her spirits and hurt her feelings? She'd put in so much hard work that he didn't want her feeling like she'd failed.

He found her in the garden training Bob to walk to heel under the shade of the cherry blossom trees.

'I thought you were going to do that earlier?' he said, striding to her.

She smiled then looked down at the growing puppy. 'We *did* do it earlier, didn't we, Bob, but we got distracted.'

'By what?'

'A text message from my brother. He asked

where his invitation to our wedding was. In far more many words, I told him to do one. How's your morning been?'

'Boring. How did your brother get your number?'

'Who knows?' She tapped her thigh and Bob stopped at her ankle. Feeding him a tiny piece of a treat, she casually said, 'So, what boring things did you discuss at your meetings?'

'Nothing important. Just the usual staff meetings.'

As soon as the words were out of his mouth, Marcelo knew he'd made a mistake.

CHAPTER THIRTEEN

CLARA TURNED HER face to him with an expression Marcelo had never seen before.

Contempt.

'So you don't think scheming to keep me out of public life is important?'

So many curses flew through his head accompanied by such a wave of nausea that for a moment he was incapable of speech.

Since Amadeo had left, Clara had been holding herself together by the skin of her teeth and reminding herself not to jump to conclusions. Just because someone said something was true did not make it so. That was a life lesson she'd learned at far too young an age.

Marcelo's face told her perfectly well that Amadeo had been telling the truth.

'Come on, Bob,' she said. 'Time to go.'

Then, with her only friend in this whole horrid island by her side, she marched into the house and raced up the stairs to her bedroom.

She'd barely passed the threshold before Marcelo followed her in.

She wished she hadn't been looking at his face when he caught sight of her suitcases, bought for their intended honeymoon and now open on her bed, one half closed, the other open, both rammed with clothes, or she wouldn't have seen him visibly blanch.

'You're not planning to leave?' he said hoarsely. 'We're getting married on Saturday.'

'*Were* getting married,' she corrected, 'and yes, I am leaving. I gave you a chance to tell me the truth and you blew it.'

But he was still staring with horror at her packed cases. 'You *can't* leave!'

'Watch me.'

Squeezing his eyes tightly shut, he took a long, deep breath. '*Bella*, I understand why you're upset—'

'Do you?'

'You feel lied to.'

'No, I don't *feel* lied to, I *was* lied to. By you. A subtle but distinct difference.'

'*Bella*—'

'You no longer have the right to call me that any more. You can address me as Clara if you feel the need to address me as anything.'

'I want to address you as my wife. *Dio*, Clara, I wasn't scheming—'

'Don't bother trying to defend yourself. I

won't believe a word of it and whatever you say to me, I can't stay and I certainly can't marry you. You lied to me when you promised—*promised*—to always tell me the truth. You told me I was perfect as I am when it turns out you doubt my ability to fit in with your family and my ability to carry off the role of Princess and want to limit my royal engagements because of it. You told me you were having meetings with your staff when it was a family conference to discuss *me*.'

He threw his head back and closed his eyes. 'I assume it was Amadeo who fed you this poison?'

'At least he doesn't shy from the truth.'

'A version of the truth twisted to suit his own purposes. I have no doubts at all about your ability to carry off the role of Princess and I told him that, just as I told him that I will not put you through official outside functions until you've learned to relax into the role.'

'That's not how he put it across to me.'

'That's because he doesn't want our marriage to be permanent,' he said with a dose of Clara's own bluntness even though it made his heart rip to say it. 'For Amadeo, duty isn't something to be endured, it's something to live and breathe. You threaten his sense of what being a royal is. The rest of us can see you're too special for us to allow your spirit to be crushed under the weight of pure protocol. I saw what it cost you the other night before you found yourself on the dance floor and lit the place up, and I will not watch you put yourself through that again. I want you to thrive and that can only happen if you're allowed to be yourself, an alchemy of Clara and the Princess.'

'Actually, the only way I can thrive is far away from liars like you.'

Something cold and sharp was scratching at Marcelo's throat. It had risen from his chest, a strengthening cloud of ice shards penetrating through him. He was losing her, and all he could do was scramble for words to make her stay.

'Goddammit, Clara, you talk about breaking trust—what about the promise you made to me? You gave your word that you would marry me. You can't just change your mind.'

'Don't you get it? I *can't* marry you now.'

'Because of one mistake? Because you believe Amadeo's twisted poison over me?'

'No, because I've lost all trust in you. Did you know, when my father died, Andrew sat me down and very calmly explained that our father was dead. No bluster or beating around the bush. Just sat there and told me, and told me that he was now my legal guardian and that I would be going to boarding school and not to bother whining about it. I hated him but I respected him for his honesty. At least I knew where I stood with him, and maybe I should have paid more attention to his honesty because then I would never have fallen for the only lie he ever told me which was when he tricked me into going to Monte Cleure. I *wanted* to trust him and believe in him... And I wanted to trust and believe in you. I *did* trust and believe in you and that makes it all so much worse because now I will never be able to trust another word you say or trust that anything you've ever said to me was truthful, and I can't say the vows I'd prepared to give my whole heart for because they would be a lie.'

The scratching at his throat suddenly subsided. The icy shards cleared, the jumble of thoughts he'd held about Clara, built in their time together, finally putting themselves in order.

'Or are you just using this one mistake as an excuse to run away from happiness?' he mused thoughtfully, dropping onto her armchair.

Her head reared like she'd been jolted.

For a long time they just stared at each other, and the longer he gazed into the suddenly frightened brown eyes, the more convinced he was in the sense of his thoughts.

He shook his head slowly. When he finally opened his mouth, his tone was low but steady. 'You wear your emotions like no one I've ever met, but you suppress the real stuff, don't you?'

'Don't talk rubbish,' she scorned.

'You only wear the superficial happiness, because that's all you allow yourself to feel. Everything else terrifies you.'

Clara suddenly felt a violent urge to cover her ears. Backing against the wall to steady herself, she opened her mouth to tell him to shut up *right now* but no words came out.

It was the way he was looking at her that frightened her. Like he was seeing right into the heart of her in the place where no one was allowed.

Not even herself.

'All this time we've been together I've never understood how you're so able to compartmentalise everything. You refuse to get angry about things, not even your brother for selling you to a pig—you just told me how he relayed your father's death with all the calm of a weather lady, and now I know why you relay the awful things that have happened to you in that tone and it's because you don't dare even let the emotion out in your voice.'

Clara's heart was thumping so hard the beats were making her nauseous. She didn't want to hear this. She couldn't find the words to tell him to stop.

For the first time since she was a little girl, her mouth had stopped co-operating with her brain.

Frightened, she hugged her arms tightly around her chest.

'You say you're happy living on your own but fill your evenings with noise to drown the silence. You fast-forward sex scenes because you say you find them boring but I wonder if it's because you're too frightened to watch real, human connection and have to confront everything you're hiding from.'

Shut up!

Her plea stayed stuck in her throat.

'Your entire playlist is made up of sentimental love songs, but that's all the romance you allow yourself. Anything else requires risk and you haven't evolved a mechanism to mitigate the risk to your own heart, have you, so you shut it down completely. You were far too young when you lost the one person who loved you with all their heart, and everyone who should have been there to help you navigate your grief rejected you. You had to deal with it alone in a silent scream.'

Shut up!

But her scream stayed stuck in her throat. Just as it had sixteen years ago.

'You crave human connection but you're so convinced that people won't like you and will reject you that you shy away from it, and if I'd been paying better attention I would have realised this day would come the minute we became lovers because real emotion terrifies you, doesn't it, whichever way it falls. And real happiness is an emotion. And what you and I have shared is real happiness, don't ever doubt that. But you don't believe in it. You don't believe in me, and you don't believe in yourself, and so you only allow yourself to exist and not truly live.'

Frustration and sadness leached into the steadiness of his voice. 'I understand why. Everyone you've ever loved and trusted has abused your trust.'

How desperately she wanted to cover her ears but now her body felt as paralysed as her voice.

Marcelo took a step towards her. That one step was enough to make her flinch.

Close enough to stretch out an arm and stroke her face, he took in the ashen pallor of Clara's cheeks. Took in her muteness.

His words were distressing her. He could see it clearly. But if they had any chance of a future, they were words that needed to be said. They were words she needed to hear.

'You're not the only one who's been existing and not living, *bella*,' he said hoarsely.

She flinched again. Her eyes were darting everywhere but him, but she was listening. He knew it. He knew her. He loved her. And she loved him. He was certain of it. She was just too scared to admit it, not even to herself.

'I told you about the time I nearly died with pneumonia but what I didn't tell you—something I have never told anyone—is that dying didn't scare me. I was aware that I could die and I *didn't care*. I've never cared about death. My time in the military is the closest I have ever felt to happiness…until you, that is. In many respects it was a perverse happiness because much of it came from knowing my time could end at any time. Accidents happen all the time. Don't get me wrong, I didn't want to die—I didn't actively seek death—just that I was drawn to the things that could end it prematurely. I always have been. My mother always said I was born without fear.'

He paused for a breath and gazed at the bowed head of the woman who'd wound her way around his heart and then burrowed a permanent niche into it.

'You've said many times that I saved you but…' A shard of his heart broke off. 'Clara, you're the one who saved *me*.'

He heard a sharp intake of breath.

'You're the one who taught me that I could have a fulfilling life without having to throw myself off buildings or indulge in rescue missions. You're the one who taught me that I needed to accept my life and find ways to counter the boredom, to tame the tiger without stifling the essence of him. What I didn't tell you is that since you've come into my life, *you've* filled that hole in me. I can endure any amount of tedium in my life if you're by my side because you banish the tedium. You've brought sunshine into these stuffy castle walls and made it feel like a home and not a prison to me.

'I know you're scared, *bella*. I'm scared too. I'm scared I've lost you.' He faltered as another shard of his heart broke away and he had to swallow hard to get his throat working again. 'I'm going to leave you alone now. I will not try to stop you leaving if that's what you still want, but I will ask this question of you—and I beg you to look into your heart for the answer... Why do you listen to those sentimental love songs so much if there's not a part of you yearning for some of that love for yourself?'

Her shoulders juddered but still she made no move to look at him.

'I ask that because you can have that love with me, because *I* love you. I love you more than I ever believed it was possible to love someone.' His heart swollen enough to burst, he stroked a lock of her hair and took the one sliver of encouragement he could that her flinch was less than when he'd stepped closer to her. 'I love you, Clara,' he whispered, 'and I will not give up on us. I will wait the whole of my life for you. You just need to reach into your heart and believe it.'

An hour later Marcelo was the one to flinch when he heard the main door close quietly.

Holding his face in his hands, he gave in to the pain that had been steadily bleeding inside him and wept.

Clara had gone.

Clara's hotel room was the most depressing space she'd ever stayed in. Worse than school. But it was the only hotel in the whole of Ceres's capital that allowed dogs and had vacancies. Still, she cheered herself up—or tried to—by taking Bob for lots of walks, often carrying him so his little puppy legs didn't get worn out. She'd explored so much of the capital that many of the streets were becoming familiar. The only place she'd done a U-turn from was the huge piazza with the central water fountain. The memories that had hit her at the sight of it had hurt her bruised heart. It reminded her too acutely of the night she'd been brimming with excitement at the step she'd been about to take of becoming Marcelo's lover.

It made her inordinately sad that they'd never had the chance to return and get a caricature portrait done.

But other than those walks, she seemed to have lost all her energy. She didn't even have the vim to rip at the peeling hotel wallpaper by her bed. She'd lost her appetite too, something that had never happened to her before. Not just that, she should have started the process of getting Bob's passport sorted but had failed to muster the energy to do that most important thing. The ache in her heart seemed to have sucked all the life from her, and what didn't hurt just felt empty. Hollow.

When she dragged herself out of the hotel bed on her fourth day there, she realised she hadn't had a shower since she'd checked in. Or changed her clothes.

Oh, this was ridiculous! She needed to step out of this funk.

The problem was, no matter how hard she tried, squashing the pain in her heart and moving on with her usual positive attitude was proving impossible, not when the image of Marcelo was lodged so securely in her mind's eye and the words he'd said to her playing like a stuck record in her head. Not when she missed him so much it hurt to breathe.

Not even the sun on her face could lift her spirits.

She just needed to try harder, she decided. Much harder. This pain would pass. It always did. She would smother it and move on with her life.

After taking Bob for a quick run in the hotel garden, she stepped under the trickling showerhead and determinedly washed every inch of herself, then put on a clean pair of jeans and a top.

A knock on her door cut through the all-pervading silence of her hotel room.

She looked through the spyhole and jumped back in shock to see Amadeo there.

He knocked again.

She opened the door a crack and used her body as a barrier to stop Bob escaping to greet him. 'How did you know I was here?' she rudely asked as a greeting.

'I asked around all the hotels that admit dogs. May I come in?'

'If you must,' she muttered.

As the room only had one small seat, Clara perched herself on the windowsill and folded her arms. 'What do you want?'

'To apologise.'

Well, that was unexpected.

'I've treated you abominably.'

'Yes.' When he didn't fill the silence, she said, 'Well…?'

'Well?'

'Your apology?'

'I thought I had…'

She shook her head.

He nodded as if to himself then met her stare. 'I'm sorry for how I treated you. It was cruel and I behaved as you rightly called me, as a pompous ass. I make no excuses. I didn't think you were right for Marcelo or for our family.'

The mention of Marcelo's name made her bruised heart flutter. 'Does he know you're here?'

'No. I thought it best not to tell him. He's not in a good place. He still hasn't cancelled the wedding. He can't let go of the hope that you'll come back to him.' His eyes narrowed and his speech slowed. 'I thought he was in denial, but now I see you, I think I'm the one who's wrong. You look terrible.'

Her heart was fluttering madly now.

'Thank you,' she croaked.

A faint glimmer of a smile appeared. 'He looks terrible too. You have matching eye bags.'

'Have you finished doling out the compliments?'

She almost caught a glimpse of white teeth.

'Yes, I am done, but I do have one more thing to say. Against my best advice, which did result in him punching me in the stomach, Marcelo will be at the altar tomorrow, waiting for you. If you come to your senses and decide to marry him, you will find no objection from me. I will welcome you into our family as I should have done from the start.'

Clara kicked the bedsheets off for the hundredth time that night. The sun filtering through the cheap curtains told her it was now morning. She didn't know why she'd bothered going to bed at all. Far from feeling any better, she felt decidedly worse.

Bleary-eyed, she threw some clothes on, took Bob, who'd been just as unsettled throughout the night, outside, then went into the restaurant for a cup of strong coffee. She couldn't stomach the thought of food, but Bob needed to eat and the hotel was good enough to provide meals for dogs. Once he'd wolfed his food down and she'd downed another coffee, she took him for his walk and tried to muster some of her old enthusiasm.

Heading towards the sprawling woodland park that all the local dog walkers seemed to favour, she was passing one of Ceres's many churches when it turned ten a.m. Each peel of the bell made her heart shudder and her brain leap to the person whose face had kept her from sleeping.

He would, at this moment, be getting ready for their wedding.

It was a thought that made her feel wretched.

The church clocks struck eleven as she headed back to the dreary hotel.

One hour.

When would he arrive at the chapel? How long would he stand there before he gave up and understood in his heart that she wasn't coming?

It was the thought of Marcelo standing at the altar waiting for the bride that would never come that filled her head as she trudged up the hotel stairs to her room. It made her heart hurt, made it *bleed*, and as she opened her door she stepped into a pool of strong sunlight filtering through the window.

Her life before Marcelo had been *happy*. She'd been relentless in her happiness, a state of mind she'd forced herself to inhabit. She'd had her job and her dogs. She'd been content with a future that consisted of being a grey-haired spinster. She hadn't felt that she'd been missing out on anything.

She'd been in denial.

Sinking onto the bed, she lifted Bob onto her lap and ran her fingers through his soft fur.

Like her canine friends, Clara had lived for the moment.

Many of the dogs at her sanctuary had been mistreated and, while they too lived for the moment, thinking no further than their immediate needs, the mental scars of their mistreatment would show themselves whenever they felt threatened. One Labrador's owner had worn black boots whenever he kicked him. That Labrador was the sweetest creature but the sight of a pair of black boots would make him cower.

Isn't that what she'd been doing? Hiding herself from all the emotional blows, cowering from anything that could truly hurt her again because Marcelo was right; she'd had to navigate the grief of her mother on her own and, not having the tools to deal with it, she'd swallowed it down deep inside her and smothered it, and then dealt with every blow and rejection that came after in the same way.

Her happiness had been a façade even to herself.

And then she'd met Marcelo.

A tear rolled down her cheek.

Marcelo...

She hadn't been looking for him but he'd found her.

The joy and happiness she'd shared with him had blown everything else away. Happiness with him hadn't been a state of mind or a decision. It had just been. That taste of real happiness...

The way he held her. The way he danced with her. The way he looked at her. The way he made love to her.

He did love her.

He'd been the one to knock down the wall she'd built to stop her from feeling true human emotions, to *smash* it down.

He loved her.

She couldn't hide from her feelings any more, she realised as another tear fell. She couldn't compartmentalise this pain. Couldn't compartmentalise Marcelo.

And it wasn't just that she was no longer capable of smothering pain. She no longer wanted to. If this was the price to pay for the joy she'd experienced with Marcelo then it was worth it. Worth every ounce of it.

And it was worth risking her whole future for… No. Not risking. There was no risk. There was no need to be scared. Not with him.

Marcelo loved her. She *did* trust that. She did trust him.

He loved her and would never, ever do anything to hurt her. Not intentionally.

With a wide smile forming on her face, Clara closed her eyes and let the streaming sun drench her skin with its light and a different form of light fill the emptiness inside her to the brim.

The light of love.

She loved Marcelo. The emptiness she'd carried inside her since leaving the castle was his absence.

She loved him and she believed in him. She believed in *them*.

A jolt of electricity blasted through her veins and she whipped her phone out of her back pocket. It was now eleven-thirty.

She made the call.

Alessia answered on the first ring.

Marcelo stood at the altar not looking at anyone. He'd not uttered a word since he'd entered the chapel. He'd refused to look Amadeo, his 'best man,' in the eye since their arrival. He'd hardly looked at him since the punch to the stomach Amadeo had invited when he'd realised the depth of Marcelo's despair. Punching him had made him feel better for about a second.

His family thought he'd lost his mind. He suspected they were right.

He understood more fully now why Clara had hidden away from her pain. The five days without her had been a pit of agony. The time had passed so, so slowly. He couldn't begin to imagine going through this torture for the rest of his life. He *had* to believe she would come.

He had to.

But as the minutes ticked by and the chapel rang the half hour, the dread rose.

'Marcelo,' his brother reluctantly whispered, 'we need to face facts—'

He silenced him with a look. He would not give up. He couldn't.

Aware that the packed congregation were restless and whispering amongst themselves, Marcelo turned his back on them, bowed his head and prayed.

God, if you bring Clara back to me, I'll be a better man. I'll open bereavement centres for children. I'll open animal sanctuaries. I'll—

A blast of music jolted him from his prayers. What jolted him even more was the recognition. It was the song he'd danced with Clara to...

He spun around.

His mouth dropped open.

Walking up the aisle in a white dress any princess in the world would be proud to wear was Clara. She was looking straight at him, beaming. At her side, with an identical grin and in a deep green bridesmaid dress, and carrying Bob, was his sister.

He blinked vigorously, hardly daring to believe what his eyes were telling him.

She got closer.

It wasn't until she was a couple of feet from him that he saw she wasn't wearing a scrap of make-up. Her hair had been swept into a loose bun, the tiara was skewed.

She had never looked more beautiful.

For a long moment, they did nothing more than stare at each other in wonderment.

And then the beaming smile returned. 'Ready to get married then, my prince?'

He couldn't help himself. Forgetting tradition and propriety, he pulled her into a tight embrace and kissed her passionately, his senses filling with the taste and scent of the woman he'd deep-down believed he'd lost for ever.

When they came up for air, he gazed in awe at the beautiful face he loved so much. 'You came.'

Her eyes shone up at him. 'I love you.' She sighed. 'I love you so much. I'm so sorry for—'

He put a finger to her lips. 'No. You are here.

That is all that matters, and you, my princess, have just made me the happiest man in the world.'

Tears welled in her eyes, but then she blinked and a flash of the old mischief suddenly crossed over her face. Marcelo thought he might just burst from the happiness that bloomed at the sight of it.

'You might want to check my feet out before you call me your princess again.'

Holding her hand tightly, he stepped back to drop his gaze to her feet.

She pulled the skirt of her dress up a couple of inches so only he could see. Instead of the traditional cream or white heels a bride usually wore, Clara had donned a pair of trainers.

'Princess Twinkletoes forgot to bring the shoes,' she explained with a giggle. 'I would have run back to our quarters for them but thought you were probably on the verge of a heart attack as it was.'

Laughing loudly, he hugged her tightly again then took her hand firmly in his and faced the bemused priest.

Without an ounce of hesitation, they both pledged their lives together.

It was the best day of both their lives.

EPILOGUE

'NOW PUT YOUR foot on the accelerator until you hear the bite.'

Something deep below Clara rumbled and roared.

'I said *until* you hear the bite,' Marcelo said with barely concealed impatience.

'But you didn't say I had to stop,' she countered, although she didn't really blame him. This was their second driving lesson in as many days, and everything he'd shown her and told her to do seemed to go through one ear and out the other.

'Not stop, hold your foot exactly where it is.'

'You should have said. I'll try again.'

This time, when she heard the bite, she smiled and said, 'What now?'

'Take your foot—slowly—off the clutch. The car will…'

The car lurched forward, cutting his instructions from his tongue.

She looked at him and grinned. 'Oops.'

He just stared at her before his face creased into a grin. And then his eyes narrowed in that expression he got when a thought occurred to him. 'Do you have any paper on you?'

'Of course not. You're lucky I'm wearing any knickers.'

That made him kiss her. Which was what she'd wanted.

He pulled back, still grinning, opened his window and shouted out at one of his protection officers. As they were at the Ceres national racetrack, a full complement of their protection were there to witness Clara's driving ineptitude.

In no time at all, a notebook and pen were being handed to him.

Curious, Clara watched as he wrote a list, admiring his penmanship. Her writing was atrocious.

Then he handed the notebook to her. 'Written instructions for you.'

She read what he'd written. A step-by-step guide to driving a car.

'Why didn't you explain it like this?' she asked.

'I did.'

'Didn't.'

He fixed her with a look. She scowled then read the instructions a couple more times before handing the notebook back to him.

Two minutes later she was happily cruising at twenty miles an hour, well aware of the smug smile on Marcelo's face.

When she'd brought the car to a stop she turned to him. 'How did you know?'

'It was a guess. I just thought you might take instructions visually better than you do verbally.'

Amazed, she found she'd lost her ability to speak.

It constantly surprised her how well her husband knew her, so well that he sensed things about her that even she didn't know.

He knew her. And, far from repelling him, he loved her.

Just as she loved him.

'I'm two days late,' she blurted out, unable to hug the secret to herself any longer.

The smug expression turned blank.

'My period. I'm two days late.'

He stared at her with that same blankness but she could see behind his ice-blue eyes to the ticking brain and knew he was making the same calculations. Clara's cycle was as regular as clockwork. In the three months of their marriage she'd never been even a day late.

The biggest smile broke out on the handsome face she loved so much and in the blink of a moment her mouth was being crushed by his.

Wrapping her arms tightly around his neck,

she kissed him back and gladly welcomed the fresh wave of happiness filling the well inside her.

Eight months later, Marcelo and Clara welcomed their first child, a daughter they named Marianne Isabella after their mothers. She was a princess in every way. Apart from her motormouth speech which developed very quickly.

* * * * *

Caught up in the drama of
Crowning His Kidnapped Princess?
Then don't forget to look out for the next installment in the Scandalous Royal Weddings trilogy, coming soon!

In the meantime, explore these other stories by Michelle Smart!

The Forbidden Innocent's Bodyguard
The Secret Behind the Greek's Return
Unwrapped by Her Italian Boss
Stranded with Her Greek Husband
Claiming His Baby at the Altar

Available now!